D0465716

DO UNTO OTHERS

A DCI HARRY MCNEIL NOVEL

JOHN CARSON

DCI HARRY MCNEIL SERIES

Return to Evil

Sticks and Stones

Back to Life

Dead Before You Die

Hour of Need

Blood and Tears

Devil to Pay

Point of no Return

Rush to Judgement

Against the Clock

Fall from Grace

Crash and Burn

Dead and Buried

All or Nothing

Never go Home

Famous Last Words

Do Unto Others

Twist of Fate

Where Stars Will Shine – a charity anthology
compiled by Emma Mitchell, featuring a
Harry McNeil short story –
The Art of War and Peace

CALVIN STEWART SERIES

Final Warning

Hard Case

DCI SEAN BRACKEN SERIES

Starvation Lake

Think Twice

Crossing Over

Life Extinct

Over Kill

DI FRANK MILLER SERIES

Crash Point

Silent Marker

Rain Town

Watch Me Bleed

Broken Wheels

Sudden Death

Under the Knife

Trial and Error

Warning Sign

Cut Throat

Blood from a Stone

Time of Death

Frank Miller Crime Series – Books 1-3 – Box set

Frank Miller Crime Series - Books 4-6 - Box set

MAX DOYLE SERIES

Final Steps

Code Red

The October Project

SCOTT MARSHALL SERIES

Old Habits

DO UNTO OTHERS

❀ Created with Vellum

For the real Angie Fisher

ONE

Back then

Angus Smart hating skulking behind the bushes that bordered the playing field, but it was a necessary evil.

He'd waited until darkness came down before venturing out of the house. He had risked a quick peek round the gap in the hedgerow but had nearly shat himself when he'd seen old Mrs McDougal coming along with her guard dog, a poodle that did a very fine impression of a Rottweiler. He'd made the mistake of trying to pet the little bastard one day and it had growled and done its best to chew one of his bollocks off.

Angus loved dogs, but this thing was a radge. And there it was, pulling on its lead, sniffing about like it was on crack, pulling her every which way, heading towards where he was hiding.

He had backed off, moving further along behind the hedge, keeping well away from the gap, feeling like he was a paedo. He'd put on his long anorak – his good Barbour one, mind, not some shite out of a charity shop – but had realised it made him look even more of a pervert as he stood there, waiting.

If the old cow let her poodle come in here for a sniff, and she followed it, he would turn his back and hope she didn't see him in the darkness. If she did, what was the worst that could happen?

'Well, your honour, I saw the defendant having a pish in the bushes. No, I didn't actually see his little dinky-do, thank goodness. It was awful. I nearly fainted, and if it hadn't been for my dog, I might not be here to tell the tale.'

That would go down well. He'd be in Grampian prison where the term 'arranged marriage' had a whole different meaning.

'No, Paul, we're not going in there,' he heard the old woman say, and at first he thought Mrs McDougal had a boyfriend with her. Angus screwed his face up at the thought, a prim and proper woman like Mrs McDougal going out with a man. Then he remembered that was the dog's name. He shuddered as he heard Paul growl and for a moment he thought the dog's owner was going to bring him in here, but they passed and carried on their way.

Trees also lined the playing fields, big, tall bastards which were good to hide behind if you were a teacher waiting to meet a pupil, like he was.

The thought of Octavia coming here to meet him made him feel like he too was a teenager, although he'd left that era of his life behind a long time ago.

Hey, steady. You're twenty-six, not sixty-six. The voice of reason mentally slapped him on the back, convincing him he was doing the right thing.

He looked at his watch and a brief wind shook the branches of the tree he was standing under, dropping raindrops on him. There had been a shower earlier on when he was coming over here, so he'd put on the raincoat he kept in the boot of his car. Then realised that this just added to the image of the deviant creeping about in the bushes.

'There's Angus-the-perv,' the locals might say if they saw him. Angus and Octavia had kept their affair secret, but it wouldn't stay that way for long.

Everybody knew everybody else's business on this God-forsaken island. That was why they were running away soon. This weekend. While Angus's girlfriend, Emily, was still over on the mainland visiting her parents.

School had broken up for the summer holidays, so the kids weren't missing anything by going over to see Woodchipper Willie. That's what Angus called his girlfriend's father behind his back, after the old man had given him the 'if you hurt my daughter, I'll kill you' talk a few weeks after she'd introduced him. Angus had laughed, thinking the old bastard was pulling his leg, but then Willie's face had gone bright red, and he'd assured Angus that he 'wasn't fucking joking; I'll put you through a fucking woodchipper', just before his wife, Claire, came back into the living room with a glass of water.

'I was only giving him the warning,' Willie had complained between splutters, feeling the chance of actually being able to crank up the machine slip through his fingers.

Claire had spoken to Angus as Willie left the room.

'Willie's very protective after...well...you know what,' she had said to him. Angus had nodded and tried to look like he did indeed understand.

4

She had been referring to 'the man we don't speak about in front of the children', a man who by all accounts should have had horns sticking out of his head. To say they had painted a bad picture of him was downplaying it.

At first, Angus had thought that his girlfriend's ex-husband really had been given the 'here, poke your head into that fucking woodchipper and see what's jamming it' treatment. But no, the man was alive and kicking, and Angus always had the feeling that he was the one who would be getting it since Willie had missed the opportunity to put his previous future son-in-law through the machine.

There was one big difference this time, though: Angus hadn't married Emily. He'd danced round the idea a few times, but his own old man had warned him that he would be paying for everything for the little brats who hadn't been 'ejected from his loins'. (That last bit had given Angus the boak. He'd been about to ask the old bastard if he meant 'ejaculated' but didn't want to know the answer.) His explanation about the kids' own father having to pay child support fell on deaf ears as his old man went off on a tangent, telling Angus that once the shag-a-thon was over and the honeymoon was just a distant light in the rear-view mirror, he'd be the one staying in on a

Saturday night looking after somebody else's kids while his wife was servicing the customers after hours in the bar where she worked.

'And she'll be driving them home in *your* car, while you're sitting at home drinking the warm dregs out of a can, trying to stay sober in case the sprogs get hold of a box of matches and burn the fucking house down.'

His old man didn't think highly of Emily.

But things had worked out fine, for a while. Then boredom had set in, and at the drama club he had shared a few laughs with one of his pupils. She was eighteen, but far more mature for her age, and in her last year of high school. They had started their relationship after she stayed back for rehearsals for a play. He was the drama teacher and had taught her more than just acting techniques. Orkney wasn't a place where you could go out and not be noticed, so they had been careful.

Their romance had blossomed, and one day Octavia had asked him to run away with her. They could go over to the mainland where nobody knew them, she said. She was eighteen. People might look for them, but they were both technically adults.

Angus had thought about it and agreed. He'd be

fucked for a teaching position again, but he would find bar work. And he had savings, something that Emily wasn't privy to. She would only have spent the money on her horrible offspring if she'd known. He would just make sure they didn't move to the same town where Woodchipper Willie lived, and they would be fine.

He was excited and anxious, waiting for Octavia to turn up and tell him that her parents had left. They and her younger brother were going to visit a relative on the mainland who was poorly. They would be away for the whole weekend, giving her and Angus plenty of time to pack and leave.

He paced up and down, wincing once again at the raindrops falling off the trees onto him, and for the millionth time he looked at his watch.

She was late. Just like she'd been late fifteen minutes ago. All sorts of thoughts were shooting through his head: she'd changed her mind; she'd told her father, who was now polishing his shotgun; she'd decided she wanted to be a nun.

All of them were possibilities, but the first one was the one he'd put money on if he was a betting man.

He stepped out from the big tree that was pissing

raindrops down on him and walked to the break in the hedgerow, looking each way to see if mental Paul-the-Poodle was gone, and when it was safe, he walked along the footpath to the car park.

Octavia lived only a short distance away by foot and he had thought about just walking, but he didn't want to leave his car up here.

He would go down to her house and see if she had bottled it. He was standing in the car park, on the periphery of a play park, and after dark or not, he would still look like a pervert if somebody saw him. A grown man lurking by a play park whether it was light or dark more often than not would result in an arrest and a wee spell on the register. Try getting work after that. He would be lucky to get a job as a lollipop man after that, but his life as he knew it was going to change.

Now he wished he'd told her he would drive up to her door, get her to jump in and they would be off, but oh no, cloak and dagger it was.

Octavia was worth it. They planned to get married on the mainland and they would start a family right away. Yes, he was only twenty-six and he could father children probably till the day they screwed the lid down, but did he want to be playing football with his kids when he was knocking on retirement age? No.

He looked at his watch again. Christ, she was thirty minutes late. Had she changed her mind? That would be messed up, especially since she had been the one who had begged him to run away with her.

Five minutes' drive down the road, he parked in Cromarty Square. He got out and walked quickly down to Front Road. A propellor sat on its plinth, looking out across the dark water.

Before he turned into her street, he wanted to make sure her folks hadn't got home early. Maybe they'd caught her and were interrogating her now and her father was gathering the troops so they could hunt Angus down and give him a good kicking.

He stopped at the end of her street and looked round the corner. She had told him what kind of car they had, and it wasn't there. He walked quickly along, looking like he had maybe come from the inn on the corner, and approached her front door with trepidation. The houses were terraced, and hers was opposite a little craft workshop.

He'd bought disposable phones for them to communicate with and he took his out now and hit the redial button, hoping she'd kept hers on. Then he heard a phone ringing and noticed for the first time in the darkness that the front door was slightly ajar.

Had her parents come back early and a fight had ensued? Why was it so quiet inside if that was the case? Maybe Octavia had been on her way out and had turned back because she had forgotten something? Obviously running late, but now she was about to fling the door open, see him standing there and jump into his arms. Christ, no, she'd shite herself and probably let out a scream.

He nudged the door open with his shoe. It swung open silently. He was about to shout out her name, but what if her father was a distant relative of Woodchipper Willie's and ending somebody's life ran in the blood? He knew her father's name was Andy, so maybe his nickname was Andy the Axe. The last thing Angus wanted was to get into a fight with her old man. Where would her loyalties lie if he chinned her dad and put him on his back? Blood and the clichéd comparison to water.

He listened carefully as he stepped over the threshold. That was it, he was in now, no going back. There was no way he could explain his presence here.

He walked along the narrow lobby, wishing he knew which door led into the living room. Luckily, the door on the right was open and a small lamp was on. He could see a chair and TV – not switched on – and he risked a peek, just a quick in and out, ready to run like fuck if her old man was in there sharpening his axe or any other implement of death.

Orkney wasn't exactly lawless, but neither was it a bustling cosmopolitan place. The lack of police meant that sometimes problems were solved 'in-house'.

The under-cabinet lights were on in the kitchen. That too was empty. Now Angus stood at the bottom of the narrow staircase. Traditionally, a serial killer would be waiting at the top, Andy the Axe notwithstanding. But so was Octavia. Unless the open door was an indication that she had either already rushed out or had left and had forgotten to lock the front door. And a gust of wind had blown it open.

What if that theory was right? What if she was already up at the park waiting for him, thinking that he had changed his mind? Here he was, fannying about in her house, and she was about to call her best friend and tell her what a bastard Angus Smart was.

He rushed up the stairs, announcing his presence with his size twelves. 'Octavia?' he said, not

11

shouting but not whispering either. It was now or never.

The bathroom was empty. The first bedroom – Ma and Pa's, with a quilt that looked like it should be in a museum, or a bin – was also devoid of life.

So was the next bedroom. Octavia's. Devoid of life because Octavia was lying naked on her bed, her dead eyes open but seeing nothing now. Blood was everywhere, jets of it having left her slashed arteries to spatter on the walls, the carpet, her bedcovers. Octavia herself.

Angus couldn't breathe. He tried, but his throat was stuck somehow, and it took a few tries for air to get in.

He could feel a sense of panic, like the time his mother had fainted in their living room and his father was too pished to help, but then Angus had taken a deep breath and somehow taken control and got his mother to come round.

This was like that time, but on a whole new level. He barely managed not to piss himself, and his instinct was to rush in and feel for a pulse, but her eyes were unblinking. Her throat wound had also released a lot of blood onto her sheets.

He wanted to go to her, but his legs wouldn't

move. Then a thought shot into his panicked mind: *Don't touch anything.*

He kept his hands to himself. Tears were streaming down his face now, and he was surprised because he hadn't felt them breaching the walls of his eyelids.

'Who did this to you?' he whispered in a choked voice. Of course, she couldn't tell him, but he knew that when the authorities came, they would be asking the same question. And they would have a number-one suspect, when it all came out in the wash. They'd been careful, but he couldn't guarantee nobody knew about them.

TEACHER SLAYS PUPIL HE WAS PLAN-NING ON RUNNING AWAY WITH

That's what everybody would think. After all, who else would commit this heinous crime? Well, somebody fucking well had, and it wasn't him.

Angus managed to tear his eyes away from Octavia. He didn't want to, but he knew he *needed* to. He had to leave. Nobody would believe he didn't do this unless some crazed psychopath walked into the police station in Kirkwall and confessed.

No, he, Angus Smart, would be fitted up for this. 'Were you in the house, Mr Smart?' they would ask.

'Well, yes, but I didn't touch her.'

'Really now? Tell us again how you went up to her bedroom and found her dead.'

'She was just there, lying on the bed, gone.'

'Of course she was. Well, we don't believe you, her parents don't believe you – and the jury won't believe you. They'll all think you went up there and Octavia told you she'd changed her mind about running off with some old shagger, so you killed her. You're well fucked, mate. And you will be when you're a new member of the Grampian Paedo Ensemble. Are you musically inclined? Because you'll be playing a lot of clarinets...'

Angus thought he was going to be sick, but that was all he needed. He'd read about how they could take a carrier bag of pish and get DNA from it. It was all science fiction to him, how they could do that, but he knew he would be nailed if he puked up here. So he concentrated and kept his dinner down.

He walked quickly back down the stairs, not booting it down in case he fell and broke a leg. That would be unscrewing the lid on the biggest can of worms. He made it back along the lobby to the front door, and felt more scared than he had before he stepped over the threshold into the house a few minutes ago.

What if somebody saw him coming back out? He

would be fucked. He stuck his head out, looked both ways and saw exactly what he'd seen when he came in: nothing. He tucked his hand into the sleeve of his jacket and pulled the door handle that way, listening for the click of the door closing.

He walked away from a scene of carnage, from the young woman who was going to be the start of his new life, away from life as he knew it.

Keeping his head down, he made it back to his car unseen; at least, if anybody *was* peering out, he didn't see them and there was nobody on the street.

He got into his car and made a quick phone call to the one person he could trust in his whole life. After he was done, he slowly drove away, his mind hammering along like a steam train. Where was he going to go? He knew he couldn't go back home. Emily and the kids would be there, and she wouldn't lie for him. At least he didn't think she would, but even if she did and told the police that he had been in with her all evening, what if one of his neighbours saw him coming and going? Those tossers would throw him under the bus in a heartbeat. Then what if Emily said, 'No, officer, he wasn't with me. He was out and came back in all moody and furtive looking?' He wouldn't be able to explain where he'd been, and before he knew it, he would be the Beast of Orkney, up there with the Yorkshire Ripper. What if they found out he had written to Jim'll Fix It when he was a lad? That would seal the deal right there.

He drove south, keeping his headlights off, just keeping the sidelights on. He spotted headlights in his rear-view mirror, the car coming up fast.

He put his foot down and didn't look back.

'I wish they would hurry up. I'm bursting for a pish,' Dodger said from the back seat of his father's car.

'Christ, will you fucking belt up?' said his father, Morris. 'I told you not to have too many before the funeral.'

'Aye, Dodger. I told you to just have one, like us,' Desperate said from the front passenger seat. Dodger's brother.

'And you can zip it as well,' Morris said.

Desperate chuckled and looked ahead through the windscreen, watching the scenery go by very slowly as the hearse took its sweet time heading for the churchyard.

'Here,' he said suddenly, whipping round in his seat.

'Sake,' Morris said, jumping a little before tutting, thinking he'd run something over.

'Did you read about the woman they buried and she wasn't dead? It was hundreds of years ago, and there was a disease in this wee town somewhere in America that made the people look like they had died, then one woman came round before they had a funeral. This guy realised that he had buried his wife but she might be alive, so they dug her up. By then, though, she really was dead. And there were scratch marks on the inside of the coffin as she'd tried to claw her way out.' Desperate turned back to look out the front.

'Away and don't talk pish,' Dodger said.

'It's true, son,' Morris said. 'I saw it on one of those shows from America. She wasn't actually dead.'

'Jesus. I hope old Bob McArthur stays down there. Imagine the old bastard getting out of his coffin before the gravediggers managed to fill the grave in and he was seen wandering about the town,' Dodger said.

'Aye, I'd shite myself,' Desperate said.

'So would you, Dad,' Dodger said.

'Would I hell. I'd just smack him one.'

'What if he came into your hoose in the middle of the night, though?' Desperate said.

'Right, that's enough of this shite.' Morris pulled into the car park, which was basically a strip of land covered in gravel in front of the churchyard. The new cemetery had been fenced off and the grass cut in preparation for its first customer. Which wasn't Bob McArthur. He was going in beside his wife, who had left him behind a good few years ago.

The first new grave was going to be for a young girl whom nobody knew was dead yet.

'I wonder who's going to be the first one in there?' Desperate said, nodding to the new cemetery.

'You, if you don't shut up,' Morris said as they all got out into the sunshine. A wind whipped in off the sea, blowing wigs and thrashing comb-overs, disturbing previously neatly brushed hair, as other mourners piled out of their own cars.

Two other young men, teenagers entering adulthood who were friends with Dodger and Desperate, got out of the back of another car. They'd been driven there by Jelly Bean's uncle, an older man who had taken Jelly Bean in after his parents had been killed in a car crash on the mainland years before.

'I wish I'd gone to the lav before we left the pub, but old Uncle fucking Fester was hurrying me,' Jelly

Bean said, looking around to see he hadn't been heard. The oldest of the group and the tallest, he smirked at the others.

'You should have been like me and had a short,' Whizz said.

'The only short you've got –' Dodger started to say, but Morris cut him off.

'Decorum, son. I know you four are going to university and people from round here will think you're all rocket scientists, but at least be rocket scientists with a bit of class, eh? An old man's about to be lowered into the ground.'

'Sorry, Dad,' Dodger said, and stuck two fingers up at Whizz when his dad turned away.

'I saw that, ya wee bastard,' Morris said, not looking round. The others laughed but kept it down.

After the service round the grave, people chittered as the wind continued its relentless pursuit of them. The older folks stopped to talk to the minister, so the group of young men walked down towards the shore and the Millennium Stone.

'I never knew the old boy, but my dad said I should pay my respects,' Dodger said.

'We're all family on the island,' Jelly Bean said. 'When one of us goes, we need to pay our respects.'

'Aye, you never know when it's going to be your time,' Whizz said.

'This is all very depressing,' Desperate said. 'I wonder if anybody would notice if I had a pish behind the stone?'

'Och, away with yourself,' Dodger said. 'Besides, we're going back for a wee shindig to celebrate the old boy's life.'

'I don't know if I can hold it that long. I hope dad's going to get the boot down going back. Fuck the hearse.'

'Hey, what's that?' Jelly Bean said.

He was standing there pointing to what he thought was something that had washed up on the shore, and then they all saw it was a pile of clothes with a rock weighing them down.

'Who do they belong to, I wonder?' Dodger said, stepping over to them. A pair of trousers and a white polo shirt.

'Have a rake in the pockets,' Desperate said. And Dodger did just that. He found a wallet and took it out. There were only a few notes in it, but there were credit cards. He took one out and read the name before looking at his friends for a moment.

'Well?' Whizz asked.

'Angus Smart,' Dodger said simply.

Morris came walking over. 'You boys ready to go? I'm starving. I hope it's a good scran. What's that?' he asked.

Dodger handed over the credit card and Morris looked at it before looking at the pile of clothes then out to sea.

'I think I should call the police,' he said, looking for a dead man and seeing nothing.

Then he called the police and started the ball rolling.

TWO

Now

'Santa Con? What next? Tooth Fairy Fest?' Detective Chief Superintendent Davie Ross shook his head and took another huge swallow of his pint.

'Oh, come on, Davie, they're just having fun,' Joan Devine said. She and Ross had been friends for years, he as a rising cop and she as a deputy fiscal. They were sitting in a bar in a lane in Glasgow city centre.

'Aye, I suppose, but do they have to be so bloody loud?'

'Christmas is knocking on the door. Everybody's having fun, except you.'

'I think all of the fun has gone out of me, Joan.'

Joan finished her drink and put the glass on the table. 'Another one? Or is your wee nightgown heating up by the fire, waiting for you?'

'You're funny, I have to admit,' Ross said, finishing his pint and putting his glass next to hers. 'I should let you buy the next one, just for your cheek.'

'I can, Davie,' Joan replied, pretending to go into her handbag.

'Aye, it's about time those moths got a wee bit of fresh air.'

Joan laughed as Ross got up from their table and walked up to the bar.

'Same again, Tam,' he said to the barman, then he leaned against the bar, looking at the bunch of scruffy bastards with their Santa suits on. This was another one of the American imports he didn't like, Santa Con. He had a friend over in the States who'd made the mistake of going down on the train to New York City on the same day that thousands of revellers were dressed as Santa, and when he got back to the station car park, some bastard had reversed into his car.

Somebody bumped into Ross just as he picked up the two glasses. The beer spilled out of his glass onto the floor, narrowly missing his trousers. He turned round to the man dressed as Santa.

'Fuck's sake, watch where you're going.'

The Santa laughed behind his beard. 'Sorry, Chief. Let me buy you another.'

'Naw, it's fine, just be fucking careful in future.'

'Aye, I will. Merry Christmas.' The Santa clapped Ross on the shoulder as he walked back to the table. He put the glasses down just as another barman came round and took their empty glasses away.

'Did you see that clumsy bastard?' he moaned as he sat down.

'What happened?' Joan asked.

'That guy bumped into me and I spilled my beer. I nearly looked like I'd had a pish without leaving the bar.'

Joan giggled. 'Who was it?'

'Him over there.' Ross nodded but couldn't pick out the Santa who'd bumped him. 'One of them.'

'You've had too much if you're seeing multiple Santa's. I only see one.'

'They call that gaslighting somebody,' he said, but smiled.

'Whoa, hold the front page; Davie Ross just

smiled.' Joan laughed before lifting her glass to her mouth.

'You're so funny, Joan Devine.'

'I can only try, Mr Ross.'

He gulped at his pint like it was going out of fashion. He'd always been a big drinker and had had a big belly to show for it for the longest time, but his wife had died and after a while he'd found he needed the company of a woman but lacked confidence. He could chew any of his staff out, or get in the face of any prisoner, but talk to a woman? He'd forgotten how to.

Then he had started looking after himself and dropped weight. One night in the bar, he'd bumped into Joan and had started talking to her and they'd hit it off. He'd known her professionally for years, but not in a social capacity, and he found he liked her company.

And they'd been friends with benefits since.

Like tonight. They'd had dinner at a Chinese restaurant and come here for a few drinks, and later they'd head back to Joan's place for a glass or two of wine and see where the evening went after that. Sometimes something happened, sometimes it didn't. Sometimes they talked. If Davie Ross had learned one thing, it was to be a good listener.

'I know it's a few weeks until Christmas, but would you like to come round to my place for dinner?' Joan asked.

Ross smiled. 'Aye. That would be smashing. Thanks. I'll be seeing the wee yins in the morning, you know, Grandpa giving them their gifts, but then I'm all yours.'

'Your daughter won't be disappointed if you don't have dinner with her and her family?'

'What? Sharon? Naw. Don't get me wrong, but it's going to be like an Ed Sheeran concert in her house on Christmas Day. The bairns will be wanting to play with their toys and this old fart will only be another body to stumble round.'

'Right then, that's settled. I usually eat around one, and then put my feet up in the afternoon, watch the Queen's speech. Although it'll be the King's speech now, I suppose. Then have a few drinks and watch a film or two.'

'Sounds good to me.'

Ross knew Joan had never married and nor did she have any children of her own. She'd been engaged a long time ago, she'd told him, but the guy had cheated on her with her best friend. She'd kicked him out and he had married the friend instead. Ginger-heided bastard.

'I was thinking that if you have any holiday time coming to you, then we could go to Tenerife for a week in the New Year. I haven't been there for years.'

'That would be great. I'll have to buy some new swimming shorts. I don't think those skinny wee things would fit me anymore.'

'I'll have to get a new outfit too. I go swimming at the health club, but something nice for Spain might be in order.' She slipped an arm through his and pulled him closer. 'I think we should drink up and get back to my place soon.'

'I think you might be right. Getting past my bedtime.'

She laughed and elbowed him in the ribs.

'Don't count on getting much sleep tonight, Davie Ross.'

He blew out his cheeks before blowing the air out of his mouth. 'I'm flabbergasted, Ms Devine. I mean, is that all it took? Another voddy?'

'Hell's teeth, I just gave my secret away.'

He laughed and they polished off their drinks and then stood and squeezed past a small group of rowdy Santas.

'In my day, you would take the kids to sit on Santa's lap and they would get a wee pressie. Nowadays, Santa's in the pub getting blootered and telling you to go fuck yourself. Aye, times change, and no' for the better.' He grabbed their coats from the wall rack and they put them on before stepping out into the cold night air.

'You fancy going up to George Square to see the lights?' Joan asked.

'Aye, that would be great.'

'We should hop on the train and go through to Edinburgh to see their market as well.'

'Sounds like a plan.'

They walked down the road, Joan putting her arm through his again. 'I'm really glad we hit it off, Davie.'

'Me too.' He smiled at her and felt comfortable. He didn't think he'd ever feel comfortable again after his wife's death, but Joan had made him see there was more to life than sitting in front of the fire after a hard day of chasing down the scum of the earth.

Springfield Court was a narrow alley that would take them out to Queen Street, where they could walk up to George Square.

As they got to the end of the lane, turning towards the entrance to the Ted Baker store, a Santa walked towards them. The red-suited man bumped into Ross.

'Fuck's sake –' Ross started to say, but then he felt a searing pain in his side and he felt his legs giving out as he was shoved and he landed heavily on his back, crashing into some wheelie bins.

Santa stepped forward and bent down as Joan gave out a shriek.

'You and that bitch Lynn McKenzie should have kept your fucking nose out of it,' Santa said, baring his teeth. 'She's fucking next.' Then he brought up the knife again, the one that had slipped into Ross's side. The one that was going to end his life.

Ross, lying on the cold ground, felt the searing pain increase and an image of his daughter and her children sprang into his mind as he prepared to die, knowing there was nothing he could do about it. Then he heard the rattling of glass bottles.

Joan had grabbed a wine bottle from a pile in the large wheelie bin whose lid had long since departed for perhaps a warmer clime, and she hit Santa full force on the arm just as he was bringing the knife down towards Ross.

'Oh, ya bastard!' he said, then stood up to his full height. 'Fucking bitch,' he said. Joan smashed the bottle on the ground, then pointed the jagged edge at the attacker.

Santa smiled. 'Seriously? Maybe I'll just do you

both. Buy one, get one free,' he said, grinning behind the fake beard and glasses.

'Go ahead, fuck face. But bear this in mind: I've come across fuckers like you before and this won't be my first time stabbing somebody with a broken bottle.' She waved the bottle in front of her face. 'I'm going to stab this right in your willy. See how you'll be with your wife after this.'

'I'm not married,' Santa replied, advancing slowly.

Ross, with one hand on his wound, had leaned over onto his side and belted the attacker's knee with another bottle before rolling onto his back again.

The attacker turned round to face the detective just as Joan was swinging the bottle again. This time it connected it with his right wrist, sending the knife flying. He shrieked in pain. 'My knee!'

He looked like he was going to have a go with Ross anyway, even though Ross was still lying down, when Joan stepped between them, waving the broken bottle in his face.

'Hey!' a voice shouted from further along the street. 'I'm calling the fuckin' polis!'

They saw a man standing there holding his phone up to his face. Santa thought better of staying and he turned and started running as best he could, looking like he'd just shat himself.

He looked back quickly before disappearing round the corner. 'This isn't finished!' he shouted, but Ross wasn't listening.

'Stay with me, Davie,' Joan shouted at him, crouching beside him with her phone out, the broken bottle nearby, and she wasn't taking her eyes off the lane that Santa had just run up. Ross was closing his eyes.

'Stay awake, Davie,' Joan said to him, then she was talking to somebody else.

But Ross couldn't stay awake.

THREE

Barney Cheetham was a world-class killer. By his own standards. He was one of the fastest ninjas ever known to man. He could almost kill by using his breath, something that those closest to him could testify to. Barney was lightning fast, which he was proud of. He was about to run the sword through one of his enemies when his bedroom door opened and he pulled his headset off.

'Ma!' he shouted, throwing the game controller down.

'I made you a nice cup of tea.'

'You could have left it downstairs. I'll be down in a minute.' He was sitting in his vest and Y-fronts.

'You don't have to be shy. I wash the things after all.'

Thirty-six-year-old Barney tutted and stayed on his gaming chair, facing away from her and craning his head round like Linda Blair.

'Thanks. Can you put it down on my dresser?' He noticed she was carrying two cups and hoped she wasn't thinking of joining him. 'Who's the other one for?'

'Your pal.'

Barney was about to blurt out he didn't have any pals, but he bit his tongue. That little nugget would have led into his not having a girlfriend, a conversation he didn't want to have. Again.

'He's in there,' his mother said after putting the cups down and leaving the bedroom. Barney's friend and fellow security guard Nigel Keith appeared round the doorframe like he was the next act who had just been introduced.

'A'right, mucker?' Nigel said, coming into the room and closing the door behind him.

'Fuck's sake, I've only got my skids and vest on. You could have waited downstairs,' Barney complained.

'And miss the *King Fu* show? I wouldn't dream of it.' Nigel was five-six in his socks and couldn't fight a burning newspaper with dog shite under it, but he was a good lad to work with. And to play online video games with.

'I was just warming up for the game tonight,' Barney replied, getting up out of his chair and grabbing his uniform shirt and trousers, then starting to get dressed.

'Aye, SkankyBaws57 can go and shag himself. Tonight, we'll show him who's boss.'

'That moniker might be a fake, to throw us off. What if it's a lassie?'

Nigel spluttered on his tea.

'Christ, you've just sprayed my fucking duvet, ya dingdong. If my old dear comes up here when I'm at work, she'll think I pished the bed...' Barney was about to add *again*, but caught himself in time. It wasn't as if he pished the bed all the time, only when he was blootered and his brain rang the alarm bells but his arse didn't get the message and get him out of bed. He'd bundled the sheets up and put them in a bin liner the last time and had pleaded ignorance when his mother complained she was missing a sheet set.

'I nearly choked there. I hope you were ready to jump in with the CPR,' Nigel said to Barney, wiping his mouth with the back of his hand. He put the cup down and looked around as if he was going to dry his hand on something but stuck it in his pocket instead.

'Aye, so I fucking was. That would look magic, my maw coming back in just as I had my lips on yours, me wearing only my skids. Get a grip.' Barney pulled his trousers up and buckled them up.

'So I would just die on your bedroom floor, then?'

'Too right you would. But I would have a nice wee tea for you after they set fire to you in the crematorium.'

'Sick bastard.'

'Anyway, what about all those kills last night? I was on fire.' Barney put his boots on.

'Jammy bastard.'

Barney laughed, putting on his clip-on tie, before sitting down on the bed, away from Nigel's tea-flavoured spit-fest.

'It's good, though, eh? Playing games when we're supposed to be working.' Nigel smiled at Barney, who suddenly looked up as he finished tying his boot laces.

'Christ, don't say it like that. Playing games.' Barney stood up. 'But aye, playing *video* games at work beats trying to stay awake in that crummy shithole.'

Nigel had suggested one day that they take a games console to work and plug it in and they could play online, using one of the TV monitors they were supposed to stare at all night. Nothing ever happened at the warehouse, and they had previously taken it in turns to get their heads down for a nap. But playing the games was so much better, and they could still see the monitors in case any night crawler was prowling about.

'Is it tonight he's coming?' Nigel asked.

Barney shook his head. Attention span of a chocolate lab's bellend. 'Tomorrow night, Nige. Tomorrow night.'

'Oh, aye, I forgot.'

'Right. Let's get cracking. We don't want those reprobates starting the game without us.'

FOUR

Catriona Taylor took another puff of her cigarette and blew the smoke all around the inside of the car as they drove along Lanark Road West on the outskirts of Edinburgh.

She and Dan Jenkins had left the office in plenty of time and now they were heading up the road in what Dan called the 'Fannymobile', a little Smart car that made the driver look like a fanny. Luckily, it had the name of the estate agent plastered over the side so nobody would think it was his.

'I wish I'd gone for a pish now,' Catriona complained.

'Use the toilet in this place,' Dan said.

'A two-million-pound house with a client in

there?' Catriona made a braying noise, spit flying onto the dash.

'Everybody has to pee,' Dan said.

'You know the rules: we have to tell the clients they can't use the toilets in case they take a dump, so *we* can hardly use them.'

'I won't tell if you don't.'

'Better than getting caught behind a bush, I suppose. Besides, it's too cold for that.'

They passed Catriona's local bar, Tanners, and she jokingly suggested to Dan they pop in for a quick gin or two. He laughed and kept on driving. He obviously thought she was joking, but she really would have gone in for one if it had been open and not breakfast time. She'd barely finished her first coffee in the office when she got the message that a viewing was needed and not to spare the horses. And to take Dan with her.

She wished it was somebody nice who wanted to see the house again, but it was *him*. The weirdo. He dressed like Tom Baker from *Doctor Who*, with a big scarf and a manky old hat. His beard looked like a badger's arse, his breath was honking and he wore glasses that looked like they belonged to Benny Hill.

But he was rich.

The Rolex she'd caught a glimpse of was gold and she had smiled her best smile the last time she'd been out here. He drove some clapped-out old Rover, but her mother had told her that rich people didn't need to buy some flashy car to prove something. And obviously Tom Powers had money. The house he was interested in was big and expensive, and he was offering well over the asking price, bringing it up to over two million.

Catriona wanted this sale more than anything. It would bring a big commission, and she could finally pay off those credit cards. Maybe she would be able to buy a box of eggs too. Maybe put some petrol in her car without having to take out a mortgage. Of course, Dan would get his cut too, even though she was the one doing the selling. Dan was there to take the first blow from the axe, should Tom Powers turn out to be a crazy bastard, but the old man looked like he couldn't blow out a candle, never mind go on a rampage.

She opened the window even though it was cold enough to make a brass monkey put on Y-fronts. She didn't want the smoke clinging to her clothes, making Powers think she was an old skank.

They drove past the junction that led up to Balerno High School. The wee bastards were in now, not fucking up the buses or thieving in the newsagents.

'Would you like to live up here, Dan?' she asked the young man as he leaned forward in the driver's seat like he was about to let one go.

'What? Up here in this posh pish-hole? No, thanks. I live five minutes from the city centre. And it's all downhill to Broughton when I'm reeking. You couldn't pay me to live out here.'

'Are you alright there?' she asked, hoping he wasn't about to have a stroke or something.

'Aye, I'm just looking for the driveway.' He sat up straighter. 'I mean, they all whine when their Amazon parcel turns up late, but they don't want to put a number on their driveway. Or make it stick out somehow. We're no' mind readers.'

'It's up here on the right.'

Catriona would have loved to live up here instead of in Clovenstone. She liked Clovie, but the houses there couldn't compete with the house that she was going to. A real piece of classic property, built back in the day when builders didn't have the need to show off their arse crack and stop every ten minutes for a piss and a cup of tea.

'There it is!' Catriona yelled, biting down the urge to add 'Ye blind fuck!' as Dan whipped the small car into the driveway, dispensing with any need to alert the traffic behind by putting his indicator on, and Catriona thought for a minute that she'd peed herself as Dan booted it past the open gates and into the driveway.

'That was an impressive piece of driving there, Dan,' she said, wondering if she should give herself a little spritz from the perfume bottle she carried, or let Dan have it in the fucking eyes for scaring the shite out of her.

She chose neither, just tried to get her heart rate under control and hoped the sweat on her top lip wasn't highlighting the little moustache that was there. They pulled up to the house and she looked at the digital clock on the satnav screen. They were two minutes early. Powers wasn't here yet. He wouldn't have got the bus, would he? Or an Uber?

'Doesn't look like he's here yet,' Dan said, leaning forward again and squinting through the windscreen.

Captain fucking Obvious. 'You sure you can see well enough to drive?' Catriona asked.

'Of course. I'm just having a wee squint.'

'*Squint' being the operative word,* she thought but kept her mouth shut.

Tall hedges over on the left separated the gardener's cottage from the front lawn. He wouldn't be skulking round there, would he? Christ.

Well, Dan couldn't drive a pig with a stick, but he looked like he would be able to boot old Powers in the goolies if push came to shove.

He turned the engine off, and she zipped up her puffer jacket after they got out. Dan assured her he was warm enough with only his suit jacket on, being from the generation of young men who went out on the ran dan on a Friday night wearing only a tee shirt. The sky was overcast and it was Baltic enough to make her wonder if she would actually start eating Dan if a snowstorm hit and they got cut off. She'd damn well make sure he was the first to go if that happened.

The cottage was along a little track, with more trees and hedges behind it. The seller said it hadn't been used in years, and Powers said he wanted to see it again, so here she was. With her bodyguard/chauffeur to make up the numbers and possibly prevent her untimely death.

'There's no sign of him,' Catriona said. 'The bastard.'

'Maybe he's running late,' Dan offered, always the glass-half-full man.

'Maybe he's just a fucking old time-waster.'

Maybe he was waiting inside for her, having parked his old clunker up the road a bit. Estate agents had been murdered before when going to meet a client. The famous case was when a young woman went to meet a Mr Kipper and was never seen again. Catriona couldn't tell if Powers had been disappointed to see she'd brought Dan the last time, and maybe he was hoping she would come by herself this time.

'Come on. Let's wait inside for him. I'm sure I spotted a kettle the last time we were here. Maybe there's a box of tea bags somewhere.'

'It's probably minging,' Dan complained. 'I mean, I don't want dysentery.'

Dan was a nice boy, but she doubted he could even spell his own name never mind the word 'dysentery'.

They suddenly stopped. The front door to the cottage was ajar.

Powers hadn't requested a key. Maybe the new girl on the front desk had given it to him. No, that was against policy, especially for a house of this calibre. Had Catriona forgotten to lock the front door when they left the other day? No, she wasn't new to this game. Even if the clients were yakking, she

43

ignored them when it came time to lock the front door.

But this was open.

She walked up to it and nudged it with her foot, debating whether to shout out or just go in and give the old bastard a heart attack as she crept up on him. Nothing short of his pissing his pants would suffice if he had somehow decided to help himself and get into the cottage. How would he do that without a key? She snorted as she thought about it; there were plenty of deviants who knew how to circumvent a slight obstacle such as a front door lock.

'Maybe you'd better go in first, Dan,' she suggested.

'Aye, no bother. It wouldn't be any worse than a wee pagger on a Friday night,' he said, and Catriona thought he was actually looking forward to going in and skelping old Powers.

The inside of the one-storey cottage was cold. The heating should have been left on so that the pipes wouldn't freeze. But maybe the door being open had counteracted the heating system.

No, it was freezing in here. She was getting more pissed off with this Powers joker. She was sure there would be other quality buyers ready to snap this place up. They didn't need this old wanker.

Dan obviously decided shock and awe was the way to go, and taking out his Stanley knife, he marched up the hallway to the open-plan living room / kitchen area, looking around for the old boy.

Oh God. Catriona held her breath, hoping Dan was going to keep the knife out of sight, but was dismayed when she saw he was holding it up in front of himself. Nothing she could say would explain that away if Powers was actually in the room and Dan got carried away and let him have it.

He wasn't. It was empty and cold and devoid of any signs of recent life.

She turned back down the hallway and stopped at the bathroom door, feeling a draft coming through the gap. She pushed it open and saw the bathroom window was open.

'Christ, how did that happen?' she said to Dan, looking at him as if she was accusing him. He just shrugged.

'We went round checking the doors and windows had been locked before we left the other day,' she said, careful to use the word *we* and not *I*. 'There's no I in team,' her old boss would always say, but she always thought, 'No, but there's a U in us' if the proverbial shite was about to start heading towards the fan.

'You checked it, Cat. You told me to lead Powers out while you locked up.'

Shite. She remembered that now, but she could have sworn she had locked the windows. Daft old cow.

She walked over and closed the window, locking it. Then she went back to the hall and checked the first bedroom, Dan right behind her.

And that was when her heart missed a beat. Tom Powers wasn't in there.

But somebody else was.

FIVE

Luckily, the house was big enough to have a drive and parking area for DCI Harry McNeil to get his Audi Q8 in. He'd thought about getting a Range Rover but thought that would have been a tighter squeeze.

A uniform had waved him through the gate and onto the property. It hadn't been hard to find, what with the emergency vehicles lined up outside on the main road.

He stopped next to a forensics van and a patrol car outside the main house and saw activity at a smaller house behind some hedges.

He got out of his car, going from being coddled by heated seats to being blootered by the chill air.

'Coldest December in twelve years,' DI Frank

Miller said, coming across to Harry. He was leaning heavily on his walking stick. 'Bloody well feels like it too.'

'I almost looked out my long johns this morning, but they're too much of a hassle,' Harry replied, wishing that he'd gone ahead with that plan. The wind cut through his trousers as he closed the car door.

'The scene is in the gardener's cottage. The two who found him are in the main house, being interviewed. They're from the estate agents.'

'I'm assuming it's warmer in there,' Harry said as they walked across the gravel parking area to the cottage.

'Don't hold your breath. Door's wide open.' Miller dug his hands deeper into his pockets.

Inside, forensic techs were bustling about and they put on overshoes before stepping into the hallway. The air was icy cold, everybody's breath adding to the atmosphere.

'Bedroom on the left,' Miller said.

Harry looked in and saw the man standing at the foot of the brass bed, his arm raised, holding a large knife. There was a female mannequin lying on the bed with what looked like dried blood on its throat and painted on its torso.

'It isn't what it seems at first,' Miller said, sniffing and bringing out a cotton hanky to wipe his nose.

Harry waited until a tech was finished what he was doing, and he saw pathologist Kate Murphy over at the other side, crouching down, looking up at the man. Then she stood up.

'Morning, Harry,' she said, smiling at him. She was wearing a disposable forensic suit, the hood pulled down.

'Morning, Kate.' Harry slowly walked round the side of the man, looking at him carefully, ignoring the mannequin for now. He was wearing a suit that looked like something Harry's grandfather would have worn, the 'demob suit' that he imagined the old man had been given after the war, based on one of the many stories he had told, whether from memory or imagination.

It was obvious that the man had been dead for a little while. His skin was the colour of milk that had gone bad a long time ago.

'Is this some kind of magic trick, where he's able to stand?' Harry asked.

'It is,' Callum Craig said, coming into the room. He was head of forensics. 'Have you seen those blokes on the High Street, painted silver, levitating while they're holding on to a walking stick?'

'I have, aye.'

Kate, Miller and Harry were staring at Craig now, waiting to be let into the inner circle where magicians' secrets were revealed.

'They have this pole welded to a platform that runs through their clothes and they're able to make it look like they're levitating. That's sort of what's going on here.' He nodded to the standing corpse.

'There are metal plates inside his clothes, and they've been drilled and screwed to his bones,' Kate said. 'I've already had a look. It's very elaborate. He's standing on a metal platform that's screwed to the wooden floorboards beneath it.'

'He looks familiar,' Harry said, feeling the cold grip him. He'd seen death many times, but nothing like this.

'It's our esteemed leader, as it were,' Miller said. 'Justice Minister Kevin Kennedy.'

Harry's brow furrowed. 'You sure?'

'Maybe you're needing new specs, Harry,' Craig said, smiling.

'I don't even wear specs now.' Harry stepped closer, leaning over the end of the bed frame to get a closer look, and then recognition dawned on him. 'Christ, so it is. His hair's been gelled and swept back. I've seen him on TV but not like this. How the hell did he get himself into this position?'

'I think he was helped,' Craig said.

'It's very elaborate, isn't it?' Miller said. 'Some-body went to a lot of trouble to pose him like this.'

'Let's just be glad the female is only a mannequin. It could have been a lot worse,' Kate said.

'That's true.'

'Strange thing is,' Craig said, stepping forward, 'this suit seems really old. Not just in design but in the feel of the material.' He looked around, expecting the others to jump in and chastise him for fucking about with evidence. 'I felt it through my gloves, and it just feels different.'

'It's almost like a set in a stage play,' Miller said.

'It's a new one on me,' Harry said. Then to Miller: 'Are Calvin and Charlie here?'

Miller shook his head. 'Elvis is around, doing the door-to-door with the uniforms, but the houses aren't exactly right next door. Charlie's got an appointment with a doctor this morning. That leaves Julie Stott and Lillian doing the interviews.'

Miller nodded. 'They've been in there a little while.'

'I'll call Calvin later. I'll go over and see how the interviews are coming along.'

Harry left the room and was about to turn and make sure the man with the large knife wasn't following him. A shiver ran up his back. 'Daft bastard,' he muttered to himself as he went outside.

SIX

Earlier that morning, DSup Calvin Stewart's day had started off reasonably well. DSup Lynn McKenzie, his girlfriend and Glasgow counterpart, had called him to say she had booked their holiday to Tenerife in the spring. He hadn't been to the island before and was looking forward to a little break.

He had just finished breakfast from the canteen when his phone rang and this call wasn't such good news.

'Sir, it's Jimmy Dunbar.'

'Jimmy, as much as I like hearing your voice when you tell me you've collared some deviant, this is a bit early, even for you.'

'It's about Davie Ross, sir.'

'Davie? What's he done now?'

'Got himself stabbed.'

'Fuck me. Is he alright?'

'He's hanging in there. Lost some blood and had surgery, but he's stable in the ICU. Joan Devine was there with him and helped fight the bastard off.'

'Right, let me go. I'll be through as soon as. Is he at Queen Elizabeth?'

'He is.'

'Right.' Stewart hung up and wished Lynn was here, but then a thought struck him: why hadn't *she* called him? Time for semantics later. Right now, he needed to get through to Glasgow.

The team were starting to arrive, with DC Colin 'Elvis' Presley trailing in last. 'Don't get comfortable,' Stewart told him.

'What's up, boss?'

'I'm going to Glasgow.'

DI Charlie Skellett was at his desk with his trousers round his ankles.

'Charlie, what the fuck's happening? You'd get arrested for doing that in the canteen.'

'It's no' a problem, boss. I have my gym shorts on.'

'Excuse me for being sceptical, but I can't imagine a fat bastard like you going to the gym.'

'Me neither, to be honest, but I wear them when I see the doc.'

'What happens if you go to see her and you've forgotten to put the shorts on?' Elvis asked. 'You shout "Surprise"?'

'Listen, son, mock if you must, but I wish my knee wasn't this knackered. I clobbered it again.'

'Define "clobbered",' Stewart said. 'But if it involved your wife, her nightie and keeping the light on, I don't want to hear.'

'I was in bed –'

Stewart put up a hand. 'Nope. I don't want to hear any of your fucking manky stories. I thought I'd made myself clear?'

'I was getting out of bed. After a night's sleep. Sir Hugo – my dog for anybody who doesn't know – was right between us, and of course I had six inches of bed to sleep on, and when I tried getting up without disturbing the wife, my knee crunched.'

'Fuck me,' Stewart said, screwing his face up.

'Was it like a sort of dry Frosties type of crunching noise?' DS Lillian O'Shea asked.

'Aye, something like that.'

'Lily, why are you encouraging him? He's giving me the fucking boak now. Knee crunching. Jesus,' Stewart said.

'What about a Rice Krispies sort of crunch?' DS Julie Stott asked.

Stewart spun round to look at her. 'Are ye daft? Did you not just hear me chastise the DS who's about to be demoted to working in the canteen for talking filth in the Incident room?'

'I'm just trying to picture Charlie's injury better, sir.'

Stewart shook his head and blew his cheeks out. 'Have you lot got a pool going to see who'll make me puke first? Not going to happen. You forget I worked with Charlie in Glasgow a long time ago, and if you've seen the man standing in the back of a surveillance van covered in mud and wearing only boxer shorts, it hardens you for anything. Almost. This talk of cartilage crunching is almost making me regurgitate my breakfast.'

'Magic,' Skellett said, putting his tub of powder down and rubbing the talc into his knee before putting his brace back on and doing up his trousers once more. 'I could do with a bacon roll.'

Stewart himself could burn calories like they were in a furnace and didn't carry any fat.

'What are you going to Glasgow for anyway?' Skellett asked, finishing fixing himself.

'My old boss was stabbed last night. He's in the

ICU. I have to go and see him. You remember Davie Ross?'

'Christ, aye. Good lad.'

'Some bastard knifed him, but his girlfriend helped fight him off.'

'God Almighty. Tell him I wish him all the best. Speedy recovery.'

'I will, pal.'

Stewart left the Incident room.

SEVEN

The big house had the heat going, and Lillian O'Shea made herself comfortable at the kitchen table as she put two mugs of coffee down, one for herself and the other for the older woman.

The kitchen was large, but the cabinets were dated, indicating that maybe the previous occupant had been elderly and had been moved into a care home or had died.

'Thanks, love,' Catriona Taylor said, putting her hands round the mug and heating them before taking a sip of the hot liquid.

Lillian had made sure she rinsed the mugs properly, not knowing how long they had been sitting in the cupboard collecting some communicable disease, but then she had realised that the house had been staged for selling. The kitchen could do with being replaced, but at least the dish towels looked like they weren't carrying typhoid.

She smiled at the woman, a uniformed officer standing by the kitchen door as back-up. 'I want you to take it from the top, starting with why you and Mr Jenkins were coming along here this morning,' she said, her Irish accent clear.

Catriona cleared her throat, then took another sip of coffee before looking at Lillian. 'His name's Tom Powers. He's a potential buyer and we showed him round a few days ago. Monday, it was. Then he put in a note of interest. Which means they want it noted they're interested without putting in an offer. Then he called yesterday, asking if he could see round the gardener's cottage again.'

'Had he shown a particular interest in the cottage when you were here last?'

Catriona nodded, still holding on to the mug like somebody would take it if she let go. 'Yes. He said he would like to use it as a little business centre.'

Lillian scribbled down some notes. 'Did he say what sort of business he was in?'

'He didn't go into specifics, just buying and sell-ing. He said he had customers all over the world. I didn't pry when he didn't elaborate. It's not really my place to interrogate them about their finances, as long as they have the money or the finances at the end of the day. But he seemed very keen to turn the cottage into a business centre where his staff would be based. He didn't want them in the house, he said, preferring to keep the business side of things separate from his personal life.'

'Can you describe him to me?' Lillian asked.

'He was tall, dressed funny and smelled.'

'How tall?'

'About six feet, something like that. He had boots on, though, I remember that. I asked him to remove them, but he said he had a bad back and wouldn't be able to tie them again without some assistance, so we left it at that.'

'And he was dressed funny?'

'He had an old-fashioned hat on, with a long, colourful scarf, like the bloke on *Dr Who*.'

'Tom Baker.'

'Yes, him. He was wearing a long overcoat too.'

'How about facial features?' Lillian said.

'Scruffy grey hair, scruffy beard, salt and pepper coloured, with round glasses. I can't remember if Tom Baker wore glasses or not.'

'I don't think he did.' Lillian looked at the older woman, who was maybe in her fifties, on a good day, or kicking sixty first thing in the morning without any make-up on. 'You said he smelled?'

'Yes. Stale, like his clothes were old and hadn't been cleaned in a long time. And he could have popped a Tic Tac. But I saw a flash of a Rolex, so I just figured he was eccentric and loaded.'

'How did you come to be here first thing this morning?' Lillian asked.

'He made an appointment just before we closed last night, saying he was busy today but he'd appreciate having a look around first thing.'

'Tell me what happened when you arrived.'

'Well, Stirling Moss nearly made me pee my pants as he booted it into the driveway...'

EIGHT

Dan Jenkins grinned at Julie Stott. 'Should have seen her face. I think she pissed herself a wee bit, but I had everything under control. I play video games and coming into the driveway was a piece of piss. As it were.'

'This is not a funny situation, Mr Jenkins,' Julie said, turning to look at the uniform who was standing inside the library. Hardback books sat on the oak shelves, which were built in. The books were all old-fashioned without dust jackets on them.

Julie was sitting opposite Dan away from the two comfy chairs that straddled the fireplace, which had nothing burning in it just now, but the central heating was taking care of warming the house.

'Of course not. But you should have seen her

face! I'm telling you, I wish I'd had my phone out to take a picture. That would have been right up on Facebook.'

'Let's try and focus on the fact that a man has been murdered,' Julie said. Dan looked young, maybe mid twenties, with dark hair shaved at the side and some sort of other coiffure going on at the top of his head which involved a tube of gel or a frying pan with yesterday's grease in it.

'Aye, of course. Sorry.' A grin still played around on his lips like he was a schoolboy who'd been told he was an obnoxious wee wanker but wore it like a badge of honour.

'You approached the house, parked the car. Then what?'

'Cat looked like she had swallowed a cactus. I bet she was thinking, by God Dan's a great driver. I mean, why wouldn't she? I got that wee hoor – the car, not her – through that gateway like it was a sausage being thrown up a close.'

Julie had heard the saying before used with a sexual connotation. She nodded and didn't let on about her version and waited for the young man to carry on.

'Then we were looking around for that old weirdo. He's a right rum bastard, if you ask me. Let me tell you something, my old man knew a purser on British Airways one time, and she brought him back a fake Rolex from Singapore or Hong Kong, somewhere like that. It looked great at first, but after a while it got tarnished and made his wrist go green when he was sweating. I reckon this golden oldie was wearing a fake Rolex.'

'Did Ms Taylor think the same way?'

Dan shook his head. 'No, she said it was the real thing. We had to agree to disagree.'

Julie tapped her pencil against the notepad. 'You see, in my mind, some rich people stay rich by not splashing the cash. Don't you agree, Mike?' She turned to look at the uniformed sergeant.

'My wife likes to splash the cash. That's why I'm a police officer standing here freezing my chuff off instead of lying on a beach somewhere warm.'

'You hear that, Dan? Mike's freezing his chuff off because his wife likes to spend some money. Like me. I like to have a wee drink with some friends at the weekend after having a browse in Harvey Nicks and buying some stuff at Marks and Sparks. I'm also sitting in this old house talking to a complete stranger instead of sunning myself on my rich boyfriend's boat somewhere warm. My point being, us working-class Joes know naff all about saving and investing, whereas the rich toffs know how to control their money, so they might buy a fake Rolex.'

Dan sat back in his chair with a smirk on his face, then he rolled up his sleeve. 'See this? Omega Seamaster 300M diver's watch. Cost me five grand. It's not a fake. I didn't want to be like my old man and buy a knock-off. What's the point? I mean, I'd know it's a knock-off. The man in the street will think you have a real Omega because they don't know any better, and even somebody having a good look at the fake watch will be fooled, because they make them look almost perfect, but you'll know that you're wearing a watch that cost a fraction of the real thing. I wanted the real thing. This watch will appreciate in value. And I might be wearing a shirt from Marks, but at least I know I'm wearing a real Omega. While I agree the rich try and save money, I would like to think that somebody who had real money would wear a real watch. The shoes on your feet and the watch on your wrist are two things that count when it comes to real money. And Catriona might not have noticed, but I did: Doctor Who was wearing trainers. And that Rolex was fake, trust me.'

Julie nodded. 'Let's say it *was* fake. You would know he had money by now, wouldn't you? When he wanted to put in an offer?'

Dan gave a little laugh. 'Let me tell you something. You work long hours, don't you?'

Julie nodded, wondering where he was going with this.

'So do I. I meet people who are excited about buying their first home together; I meet people who have just got divorced and are starting over again. They're the ones who get the financing and put a deposit down and do the deal. This old boy is a time-waster. He hardly said two words, and not to me, I mean. I drive Catriona as a sort of bodyguard. Just in case she comes across a bloke like this. I might not interact with them much, but I observe. And this old joker was wandering about the house like he was looking for the best place to set it on fire. He had a quick shamble around the cottage and we headed out. Then he wanted to come back today and look at it again. Dodgy bastard, if you ask me. And to think he came back and murdered somebody? I would have knocked him out if he'd started.'

'A fighter, are you?' Julie asked.

Dan was still grinning. 'I've had my moments.'

'Right, so we've established you were in the cottage and could have left a window unlocked, and come back and murdered that man.'

Dan didn't miss a beat. 'I'm sure that your

forensics people or the pathologist will establish a time of death. Come and ask me where I was at that time, and I'll tell you where I was and who I was with. If there are any holes in my timeline, maybe you and I could discuss it over dinner and a drink or two.'

Julie felt her mouth dropping a little bit before snapping it shut. Then she turned back to the uniform. 'You hear that, Mike? A meal and a drink.'

'I heard that. Meal and a drink. It certainly beats taking him down to the holding cells and smacking the shite out of him with a rubber hose.'

Dan's smile faltered. 'I just meant –'

'A man's been murdered and you're sitting here being flippant,' Julie said.

'Flippant,' Mike added, looking like he was gearing up to go looking for a hose, to save a trip to the holding cells.

'Sorry, okay? But it's like going to an art gallery: you see a beautiful piece of artwork and you feel like you can stare at it all day. I was just looking at you and felt I was in an art gallery.'

'Phhtt,' Mike said, and Julie turned to look at him before looking back at Dan. The young man certainly had a way with words.

'Did you have any contact with Tom Powers

during the week, between the time you first saw him and today?' Julie asked.

Dan still had a smile playing around on his lips. 'No. I last saw him here, and Cat was doing all the other stuff with him – phone calls, emails, the usual things she does with a client. At least I assume that's what she was doing with him. That would be the normal thing.'

Julie nodded. She had a feeling that Dan was hiding something but couldn't put her finger on it. 'Did you know the victim?'

'Have you identified him?' Dan replied, not falling for the leading question. If he had replied, 'Yes, of course I do,' then she would have asked him who he was.

But if he knew the victim, he was hiding it well behind his smile and greasy hair.

'Did Powers say what he was going to use the gardener's cottage for?' Julie asked.

Dan shrugged. 'Maybe he was going to employ a gardener. No, wait!' He snapped his fingers. 'I was trying to tune the old fanny out, and I was having a wee neb at all the shite that had been left in the cottage – you know, old magazines that were lying about. There was an old copy of a car magazine, but it looked bogging, and let's be honest, you don't know who's been and touched it. What if they'd scratched their arse and then started flipping through it? There are some manky bastards going about. Let me tell you, we were showing a couple around a house in Cramond, and the bloke bogged off for a few minutes. "Bogged off" being the operative words here, by the way. Cat did her rounds when the couple had left, making sure everything was locked, and found this manky bastard had used the lav, and not for a number one either. Christ, some of these lowlifes shouldn't be allowed out on their own, but they make it a day out, going looking at houses they can't afford. But using the facilities, that's not on.'

'Are you saying Powers used the bathroom in there?' Julie asked.

'No, he didn't. I made sure of that. But he did go in and have a look at it. Just in and out again.'

'Did Ms Taylor check the house after he was gone?'

Dan sat back in his chair. 'No. Not this time. She had me go round and check the windows in the big house, making sure they were locked, but it was different with the cottage. It was the end of the tour, and she was edging the old bellend out. He'd been in the house a long time, asking a million and one fucking questions. I was like,

69

"Hurry up, bawbag, I'm starving." Not to his face of course, but in my head. I was meeting the boys for a few beers that night, and me and Cat still had to drive back into town. I wasn't wanting to waste my time with this numpty if he wasn't going to buy the place.'

'The fake Rolex being the decider,' Julie said.

'Exactly! I thought he would be lucky if he could afford a doll's house, never mind this gaff. Anyway, we were ushering him out and he hadn't been near any of the other windows.'

'Now we think he managed to go into that bathroom, unlock the window swiftly and make you think he hadn't done any such thing.'

'He wasn't in there long enough,' Dan repeated.

'He wasn't in there long enough to drop troo, so you didn't think anything of it.'

'Correct. If he'd asked to use it, no doubt Cat would have let him, but he was in there asking about the plumbing and the shower and...I don't know what else because...'

'Because what?' Julie asked.

Dan's smiled faded. 'Because I'd answered a text my mate had sent to me about going out that night. I was distracted. But to be fair, so was Cat.'

'You hear that, Mike? Young Dan here was

distracted. That wouldn't do in our business, would it?'

'That wouldn't do at all. We have to be on our game all the time,' Mike answered.

'Has anybody else come to see the house between then and now, so far as you know?' she asked.

'No. They would have sent me out with Cat if there was anybody else. She's responsible for this listing so she would get the call to come out here.'

'I'm assuming this place is viewing by appoint-ment only?'

Dan nodded. 'They wouldn't open up a place like this for the great unwashed to just walk in and start chorying things.' He looked at Mike. 'People steal stuff from houses and you lot do bugger all about it.'

'We have a lot bigger things to deal with than somebody nicking a carriage clock out of a musty old hovel,' Mike answered. 'Like dealing with murders.'

'Present company excepted,' Dan now said to Julie with a wink.

Christ, she thought. She didn't have a boyfriend at that moment, but this young guy was giving her the boak. Was he really, though? He wasn't bad-look-ing, had confidence and was probably good fun.

He could also be a killer. She shook her head, mentally, and moved on.

'We're going to need fingerprints and a DNA sample,' she said. 'One of the techs will get them from you.'

Dan shrugged and made a face as if this was no big deal. 'Bearing in mind my fingerprints are in the house, pre-murder, and my DNA will be all over the place, so my solicitor would shoot that down in flames...no, I would go with motive if I was you.'

Julie wanted to reach over and slap the bastard. Being a smartarse was one thing, but Dan took it to a whole new level.

'You hear that, Mike? Motive. What do you think?' She turned round in her seat, eyebrows raised.

Mike nodded. 'Young lad's got a point there. Motive would be a good thing. But if you did find his DNA in the bedroom, on either the victim's clothes or near the body, we could just frame him for it. Close this case and you earn some brownie points. He'll be whining like a wee lassie of course, like they all do when they get sent down, but nobody will believe him. And then some of the boys down in Saughton will want to have a one-on-one conversation with him, with a pillow to keep him quiet. Yeah, I would fit the bastard up if it was up to me.'

'Hey, I'm still in the room,' Dan said.

Julie turned back to him. 'You hear that, Dan? Mike there thinks you'll be somebody's bitch in Saughton.'

Dan sat back with his hands up. 'Listen, Julie, I've been upfront with you and Mad Mike there. I've told you the truth. Let me assure you, I don't know what went on with that Powers nutcase, and I wasn't involved in...whatever that was in that bedroom. As I said, give me a time and I'll give you an alibi.'

'Give me your details, Mr Jenkins, and we can move on.'

Dan rattled off his phone number and address.

'That was smooth, by the way. Getting me to give you my details. Dinner sometime?'

'The lady says you're done here, Jenkins,' Mike said.

'Mike's right, Mr Jenkins. You're free to go,' Julie said. 'But if you think of anything else later, give me a call. My number's on there.' She handed him a business card.

Dan stood up and leaned over the table a bit. 'Obviously, I meant dinner without Uncle Mike there.' He chuckled as he stood back up and left the room, winking at Mike on the way out.

'That was exhausting,' Julie said, standing up and putting her notebook away.

'You should have let me have a wee chat with him. Taught him to show some respect.'

'Thanks, Mike,' Julie said, patting the older sergeant on the arm.

'You're not going to go out for a drink with him, are you?'

Julie laughed. 'Of course not. I *do* need a drink, though.'

As she walked out of the room, Dan was nowhere to be seen. But Julie couldn't help imagining sitting in a bar with the man. He was about her age. *No, don't be a silly cow,* she told herself, and walked out of the house into the cold.

NINE

Calvin Stewart walked along the corridor in the Helen Street station in Glasgow and banged open the Incident room door like he was about to open fire, but he did nothing more dangerous than look around. He spotted DI Lisa McDonald over by a whiteboard and walked over to her. A red-headed young man was sitting at a computer, a young DC whom Stewart had met briefly before.

'Oh, good, look who's here for a cup of tea,' the young man said.

Lisa whipped her head round and her eyes went wide when she saw Stewart standing there. She couldn't believe what she had just heard. 'Good morning, sir,' she said.

Stewart ignored her for a second as he looked at the young man. 'Are you talking to me, son?'

'I was. I'm just pleased you're popping in for a cuppa,' he said, his tone thick with sarcasm, 'since we're not that busy. Come here to catch up again. You know, I read about that, how some people can't wait to retire but then come back. Can't stay away from their old workplace.'

'Did you now, ya speccy wee bastard? What's your fucking name?'

'Hamish O'Connor. Detective constable.'

'You might have read about how to treat a superior officer. I'm assuming you went to Tulliallan?'

'Passed with flying colours. Why? You want to swap war stories?'

Lisa started walking forward, but Stewart put up a hand. She stopped in her tracks.

'I'm going to assume your mother dropped you on that fucking ginger heid of yours when you were a bairn. Otherwise, I might wonder why the fuck you were talking to me like this.'

'Look, Grandpa, DI McDonald and I are going to have a busy day, so why don't you go and play dominoes in some old people's club somewhere?'

Stewart took a step towards the young man, who

remained seated. 'You know, I also read about how some coppers retire and can't stay away. And I read about how some coppers retire and come back to the job.'

'Really now. I've never heard of that happening.'

'Well, you fucking have now. I'm Detective Superintendent Calvin Stewart. Notice how I didn't say "ex" there? That's because I came out of retirement. You might not have heard about me coming out of retirement because I've been working through in Edinburgh for the last six months.'

Hamish wasn't sure if the older detective was joking or not and sat silently looking at Stewart. He turned to Lisa, who nodded.

Then Hamish smiled. 'Good to see you again, sir. I hope you don't mind my little prank just there?'

'If I ever hear you talking to another officer like that again, of equal or higher rank, you'll be out of here so fast your feet won't touch the ground. In fact, you'll think you have a broom shoved up your arse you'll be flying so fast. You understand me?'

'Yes, sir. Of course, sir.'

'If it wasn't all hands on deck right now, I'd see to it that you were given your fucking jotters. I told you the last time I met you that the remark you made when I was leaving would bite you in the arse. It just did. Don't fuck with me.'

'Got it, sir. Sorry, sir.'

'Get back to what you're doing. Speak when you're spoken to and pretend you're invisible.'

'Invisible. Check.'

'Joan Devine's waiting in Jimmy Dunbar's office,' Lisa said, throwing Hamish a quick look that would wilt weeds.

'Right. Thanks, Lisa, and make sure you keep that wee bastard on a tight leash. I'll give him fucking old people's club.'

Lisa nodded, having no words that would explain why Hamish had done what he did.

Stewart knocked on the door to Dunbar's office and opened it and walked in.

Deputy Fiscal Joan Devine stood up from behind the desk and came round without uttering a word and threw her arms round Stewart and began crying. Stewart held her.

She pulled away when her crying had subsided. 'Thank you for coming, Calvin,' she said, grabbing a tissue from the box that sat on the desk.

'How is he, Joan?' They sat back down, and Stewart faced her across the desk and watched as she dabbed at her eyes before blowing her nose.

'He'll live, thank God. They operated on him, but the knife wound wasn't deep and didn't do too much damage. He's going to be okay, but I'm a wreck. It could have gone the other way. Davie got lucky, Calvin.'

'Sounds like it. I called DSup McKenzie on the way over and she said there's no suspect yet.'

Joan gave him a brief smile. 'It's okay to call her Lynn. I know you've been seeing each other for months now.'

'I don't know what you mean, Joan.'

'I didn't get to work in the fiscal's office for nothing. Besides, I'm a woman. We know stuff like that. I could just tell by the look on her face whenever she mentioned your name.'

'That makes a change. Unlike that wee gingy speccy twat out there. Not many people talk about me in social circles without poking a pin into my effigy.'

'Well, we've always been friends. You're a damn fine copper, Calvin Stewart. That's why you were encouraged to come back.'

'Aye, well, Lynn and I hit it off. She comes through to stay at my place in Edinburgh and vice versa. We get on well.'

'Just like Davie and me. I've known him for a

very long time, and we just started hanging out in the pub after his wife died. We had this sort of...I don't know, natural attraction. He's going to retire next year and so am I. I've had enough of the fiscal's office. So we're going to sell our houses and move to somewhere warm.'

'Good luck to you both.'

Joan looked at him. 'Oh, Calvin, when he passed out last night after being stabbed, I thought I'd lost him. I've never felt so scared in my life. Thank goodness he wasn't stabbed again. I broke a bottle and threatened the bastard with it, then Davie thumped his knee with a bottle and somebody started shouting they were going to call the polis, so he ran off.'

'Did you get a good look at him?' Stewart asked.

'Oh, yes. Santa Claus. That's it in a nutshell.'

'Sound local?'

'Scottish, but I'm not sure if he was from around here. This Santa Con attracts people from all over Scotland. And the bloody thing lasts three days. I ask you: three days! I mean, I know there must be Christmas celebrations, but for God's sake.'

'Maybe we should head over to the hospital now?' Stewart said.

'Lynn said she would pop in to see Davie. She should still be there now.'

'She is. She was there when I called her a wee while ago.'

'Notice I didn't put mascara on?' Joan said as she stood up.

'Oh. No, sorry. But you mean you don't look like a panda like you would have if you'd been wearing it and crying. I'm sure Davie will appreciate that. I mean, we don't want to add a heart attack into the bargain.'

They left the Incident room, with Stewart giving Hamish the two fingers to the eyeballs warning that he was watching him. Hamish shrank down even more into his computer chair.

'I think we should have nicknames for each other,' DS Robbie Evans said as he and DCI Jimmy Dunbar walked along the corridor to the Incident room from the canteen.

Dunbar's mouth was full of egg roll. Evans interpreted the answer as 'Fudge doff, apples pole' and almost had to duck as pieces of roll and egg came flying out of Dunbar's mouth at the same time like breakfast roll shrapnel.

Dunbar chewed, swallowed and drank some of

his coffee to wash it down, then looked at Evans. 'I already have a nickname for you, and it rhymes with "anchor".'

'That's no' very nice really, is it, boss?' Evans sipped his own coffee. 'I'm being serious, though.'

'That's the disturbing thing about this.' Dunbar bit off more roll. They were walking along at a slow pace to give him time to eat. He swallowed some of the roll and washed it down. Rinse and repeat.

'Like on the reruns I was watching. *Starsky and Hutch*. You know, Hutch calls Starsky...well, Starsky. And Starsky calls his pal Hutch. I could call you Dun.'

'That sounds like "dumb", ya wee bastard. Shut up about this fucking nickname thing.'

'Even a superhero name thing,' Evans continued, ignoring him. 'I could be Balls of Steel, and you could be Old Fanny.' Evans grinned as they turned a corner.

'Tell you what, why don't I boot *you* in the fanny and we'll see if you really have balls of steel?'

'I was just throwing things out there, boss.'

'There's a window; go and throw your fucking self out of it. See how that works out for you.'

'Believe it or not, I know of some teams who have

nicknames for themselves,' Evans said, keeping to the middle of the hallway in case Dunbar got any ideas about helping him onto the window ledge.

'Don't talk pish.'

'I'm serious. You know Nick Walsh from drugs? They call him Nut Job Nick.'

'Not to his fucking face they don't. And they call him that because he *is* a nut job.'

Evans tutted. 'Nut job. My old maw could wipe the floor with him. He thinks he's hard because he shaves his head.'

Dunbar looked over his shoulder. 'Oh, hi, Nick.'

Evans whipped his head round before looking back at Dunbar. 'Christ. I was about to get wired into him.'

'Of course you were, son. Maybe your nickname should be Skid Mark.'

They went down a flight of stairs, Dunbar finishing his roll. He finished his coffee and wiped his face with a napkin as they walked towards the Incident room door.

'Did you hear about Davie Ross?' Dunbar asked.

'About him shagging Joan Devine? Aye, I heard about that. She must be desperate or he won the lottery or something.'

'Not that. He was stabbed.'

'Jesus. Is he okay?' Evans said.

'Luckily, he is. He had surgery, but he's going to pull through. He was with Joan at the time and she helped fight the attacker off.'

'Bastard. I don't suppose we got him?'

Dunbar shook his head. 'No. He was one of those heid-the-baws dressed as Santa.'

'Recipe for disaster that is.'

'What gets my goat is, the bloody thing's on for three days. Three bastard days of Santa's running about pished, getting into fights and causing mayhem.'

'We should have a whip-round for Davie,' Evans said.

'One of the lassies upstairs is organising that. Make sure you dig deep.'

They went into the Incident room, where Dunbar tossed his rubbish into the bin at the side of Hamish's desk. Hamish looked at the boss but said nothing.

'Morning, Lisa,' Dunbar said.

'Morning, sir. DSup Stewart was in earlier and he went to the hospital with Joan Devine to see DCS Ross.'

'Right. I'm assuming you've started work on

trying to find this knifeman?' Dunbar looked at Hamish. 'Hamish? Anything?'

Hamish looked up, his face white. 'We're looking at council CCTV and we've sent uniforms out to have a look for businesses in the area that have cameras outside.'

'You alright there, son? You look like you've seen a ghost.'

'He saw Calvin Stewart,' Lisa McDonald explained. 'And before he found out that the boss is back from retirement, our Hamish decided to call him "Grandpa".'

Dunbar looked at the DC before looking at Evans. 'Maybe we should call *him* Balls of Steel.'

'That one's taken,' Evans said.

Dunbar looked at Hamish again. 'What possessed you? Did you have a wee swally on your way to work?'

'I just thought he was some old geezer coming in to reminisce about the old days, and I remembered him being a cheeky...well, you know, the last time we met.'

Dunbar laughed. 'Our Calvin has a long memory.'

'I might as well put in for a transfer to Inverness or something.'

'You'll be fine as long as you get your head down and produce some good work. Besides, he won't be here for long. Maybe a day at most.'

Dunbar turned round to Evans and said in a low voice, 'I hope.'

TEN

'Good morning, Superintendent,' DSup Lynn McKenzie said as Calvin Stewart walked into the private hospital room with Joan Devine at his side. It was warm in the room and felt even more so after coming in from the cold.

'Good morning,' Stewart said, a slight smile on his lips.

'Oh, give over, you two,' Joan said. 'You can relax, Lynn; I sussed it out ages ago, about you and Romeo there.'

Lynn looked taken aback for a moment. 'Really?'

'Really,' Stewart said. 'I tried to bullshit her, but she was having none of it.'

'Oh well, it was bound to get leaked eventually.'

'Your secret's safe with me,' Joan said and moved

over to the side of the bed where Chief Superintendent Davie Ross lay. 'How's he doing?' Her lips quivered a bit, but she fought to keep her composure.

'The doctor said he's going to make a good recovery. They're keeping him sedated for the moment.' Lynn looked at Joan. 'He was lucky. The doctor's words, not mine.'

'He was,' Stewart said. 'We've seen many a stabbing victim lying on the steel table in the mortuary.'

Joan looked at Lynn before speaking. 'Just before Davie passed out, he said something to me.'

Lynn stood and waited for the older woman to carry on. 'I'm listening.'

'He told me what his attacker said to him. He got in close, so I didn't hear, and luckily Davie had the foresight to tell me.' She looked at Stewart to see if he was paying attention. 'He said, "You and Lynn McKenzie should have kept your nose out of it. She's next.'

Lynn stood still, keeping her eyes on the woman, like she was waiting for her to laugh and tell her it was a joke. But she didn't.

'What were you both working on?' Stewart asked.

Lynn looked at him. 'Christ, we've worked on a

lot of things. He's the boss and we go over cases all the time. I wonder what case he was referring to?'

'I didn't get the chance to ask Davie before he passed out,' Joan said. 'The thing is, I don't think it's safe for you to be in Glasgow just now.'

'I think Joan's right,' Stewart said. 'He knew you by name, so it seems a credible threat.'

'I could arrange to have you put into protective custody,' Joan said. 'I know a man who can make that happen. Or even a team from your own colleagues.'

'No, no, I'll be fine,' Lynn said.

'Listen, you've been staying at my place in Edinburgh at the weekends, so why don't you take more things through and you can stay there full time? I mean, until this threat is taken care of,' Stewart said.

'I don't want people to think I'm running away,' Lynn replied.

'Nobody will think that,' Joan assured her. 'In fact, I can have a word with the chief himself and suggest you do a temporary transfer to Edinburgh until this blows over. I mean, it was probably somebody you've arrested and who's pissed off at you.'

'What about you, Joan?' Stewart asked. 'Do you think he'll come back for you?'

'Well, way to put the shitters on me, but no, he only seemed interested in Davie. I mean, he might after I threatened him with a broken bottle, but I wasn't on his list.'

'Take care, though. You know you can have uniforms drive you to wherever you want to go.'

'I know, Calvin, thank you.'

Stewart looked at Lynn. 'We have clothes at each other's place. Why don't you go through to Edinburgh, and as Joan says, it will be a temporary transfer. I'll stay at your place.'

Lynn looked hesitant for a moment. 'You think that will be best?'

'I do. For all we know, Santa might have some friends who will pay you a visit.'

'We don't know that he has my address.'

'We don't know that he *doesn't*. The attack last night was planned.' Stewart turned to Joan. 'Did you see anything unusual? Did anybody approach you?'

She snapped her fingers. 'Christ, yes. A Santa bumped into Davie in the pub, and he was apologetic, but Davie was pissed off at him. That might have been the same guy.'

'I don't suppose Davie took photos or anything?'

Joan gave a brief smile. 'No. He carries a phone. That's the extent of his friendship with technology.'

'Did the guy bump into him close up?' Lynn asked.

'Yes, he was right against him. Spilled Davie's drink. Davie told him to watch what he was doing. The guy was nice about it and offered to buy more drinks, but Davie just told him to mind what he was doing.'

'Are Davie's clothes in that wardrobe?' Lynn said.

'Yes.'

'Do you mind?' Lynn asked, pointing.

'No, go ahead.'

Lynn stepped over and opened the wardrobe door. She half pulled out the jacket that was hanging there, making sure it stayed on the hanger, and reached into an outside pocket. Nothing there. She found it on the second try.

She brought her hand out and laid her palm flat.

'What is it?' Joan asked.

'A tracker. You know, those little things that are supposed to be used to find your keys, but perverts and scum are using them to track people? Looks like this was dropped into Davie's pocket. The attacker could follow you and you wouldn't know it.'

'Aren't you supposed to get an alert on your phone?' Stewart said.

'It doesn't kick in for a few hours. He would probably have an alert now if he looked at his phone, but not if it was dropped in just a little while before you left the pub. I think he was trying to make sure he didn't lose you so he could follow you without it being obvious,' Lynn said.

'Jesus, that's scary,' Joan said.

'What will we do with it?' Lynn asked.

'I'm sure the tech guys will know what to do with it,' Stewart said. Then he looked at Joan. 'Was the guy near you?'

'No. Just Davie.'

'Would you mind checking through your bag?'

Joan picked up her handbag and rifled through it, bypassing what Stewart thought must surely be a kitchen sink, then she emptied the bag out on the end of Davie's bed. 'Nothing there,' she said, going into an inside pocket in the bag and coming up empty. She went into her purse and didn't find a tracker there. 'Thank God.'

'What about you, Lynn?' Stewart asked.

'I don't carry a handbag on duty, or a purse. Just a wallet to keep my cards in.'

'Coat pockets?'

Lynn stared at him for a second before grabbing her coat from the back of the chair she'd been sitting in. She put a hand in each pocket and found nothing. Then she searched the inside and felt something there. She brought her fist out and opened her hand. A tracker sat in her palm.

'Jesus Christ. Where did this come from?'

'Same place that Davie's came from,' Stewart said.

ELEVEN

DI Charlie Skellett was an avid reader, plain and simple. He liked to get wired into a good book and was a fan of different genres, except maybe the books where there was a bare-chested man on the cover and the character no doubt chopped wood with his knob, but he didn't mind reading crime novels, or even some historical non-fiction.

But he drew the line at reading the magazines in the doctor's office. He looked at the sorry pile on the table in front of him and wondered what sort of disease the donor had and whether anybody had caught something from them. There was less chance of catching a pox back in Victorian times than there was from these car magazines.

'You don't know who's been touching those,' an

old woman sitting opposite said. 'My husband would never touch them. You don't know what part of them touched the pages.'

'Your husband's a wise man,' Skellett said, hoping the sanitiser really did kill ninety-nine per cent of all known germs.

'Was. My Bert's been gone seven years now.'

'Sorry to hear that.'

'Don't be. He lived a good life. We have two boys and they have kids of their own now. I don't dwell on the past, but I look forward to getting up every day and seeing my grandkids. I look after one of them. Not today of course. Have you got any kids?'

'I have a daughter. She has two kids. I see them some weekends.'

'You look too young to be a grandpa.'

'That's very kind,' Skellett replied, hoping she wasn't hitting on him.

'Do you take them places?' the woman asked.

'Aye. I'm limited nowadays because of my knee, but we get around.'

'There's a *Dr Who* exhibition on at the museum next week. I'm taking my grandkids to see it. Yours might have fun there too.'

'Maybe I'll check that out. Sounds like fun.'

The waiting room in the orthopaedic outpatient

building in Lauriston Place was like any other in a medical establishment, with posters on the wall advertising some medical advice. One showed the anatomy of a knee, giving Skellett the boak.

'Do you remember the Princess Margaret Rose Hospital up at Frogston?' the woman said. She was wearing a thick overcoat and it was still buttoned up, making Skellett sweat even more just looking at her.

'Aye, I do that.'

'My Bert went there once, before they closed it and built houses on it. Do you see the irony of living in Edinburgh? We knock down hospitals and build houses on the site, and now you have a lot more people but there's not the facilities for them. They transferred the service to the Royal Infirmary. God forbid they should keep hospitals open.'

'Mr Skellett?' a nursing assistant said as she stepped into the waiting room.

'Yes, that's me,' he said, struggling to stand up, leaning heavily on his walking stick.

'What's your first name?' the old woman asked.

'Charlie,' he said.

'I'm Florence. Nice meeting you. Hope your leg gets better. Have fun at the museum.' She smiled at him.

'Thanks. I hope you get better too.'

He hobbled along the corridor to an office, where he was told to wait for the doctor, cursing himself for getting the theme tune to *Dr Who* stuck in his head. *Woo-ooo-ooo. Fuck.* He sat down and was left alone for ten minutes until the doctor came in.

'Mr Skellett, good to see you again.'

'Dr Jenkins. Likewise.'

Jenkins sat behind his desk and opened a folder and pulled out a sheet of paper. Then he looked at the detective.

'Are you going to have to cut it off?' Skellett asked.

Jenkins grinned. 'I won't be cutting anything off. I was looking at the results of your MRI and the radiologist said there was a minute tear, but I'm not seeing that. There's a slight shadow in there, but not what I would consider a tear. Now, I *could* go in and have a look, but it might make your knee worse. It's no guarantee that it would fix anything. You knee looks in pretty good shape for your age.'

'What about the numbness in my leg?'

'That usually indicates nerve damage. You might have damaged the nerve in your knee when you fell and landed on it, but so far none of the doctors have been able to give you a definitive answer.'

Skellett blew out a breath. 'So I'm stuck with it for the time being?'

'We can have you try physiotherapy, but basically, yes. Maybe pain management, where a doctor would give you an injection of an acid formula, but that's not always a help.'

Skellett nodded. 'Thanks for your help, Doc. I'll just wait and see if it gets better on its own. I don't fancy being opened up right now.'

'As you wish, Mr Skellett. Just don't go doing any marathons anytime soon.'

Skellett stood up. 'No fear of that. I can barely run to the toilet.' He fist-bumped the doctor and left his office. When he got into the waiting room, old Florence was gone.

TWELVE

'You're going to be fine, sir,' DS Lillian O'Shea said to Harry as she stood next to him in the mortuary. He hated the smell of the place, so much so that it made him feel sick and like he was going to faint. Normally, he would delegate this bit to one of the team, but this was such a strange victim, he wanted to come along.

Frank Miller was standing on the other side of the table, grinning.

'Of course I'm going to be fine,' Harry said. 'Why wouldn't I be fine?'

'Because you look like you've seen a ghost.'

'I'm just hot, that's all. I'm fine being in this place now.'

Miller still had the smirk on his face.

'Bog off,' Harry mouthed and shook his head. Already he could feel his breakfast cereal buying a return ticket.

They turned round as the mortuary assistants wheeled in the victim and manoeuvred him onto the table. He was in the same pose he'd been in when he was standing in the bedroom of the cottage.

'Smells musty,' Miller said. 'At least it's better than the smell this place has.'

Harry shot him a warning look.

Kate Murphy and one of the other pathologists, Finbar O'Toole, took the jacket and trousers off the victim with help from the assistants.

They got a closer look at the pieces of metal that were screwed into the bones of the victim. He had obviously been dressed in underwear and a shirt before the metal was attached.

'This would make it easier than attaching them first and then trying to dress him,' Finbar said.

'This doesn't look like some clumsy attempt to make him stand,' Harry said.

'If this was his first attempt at doing this, then it was a brilliant job,' Lillian said.

'Anybody seen anything like this before?' Kate asked.

They all shook their heads at once like it was a synchronised competition.

'Nothing remotely like it,' Harry said.

Kate and Finbar got to work, unscrewing the plates with little electric drills until all the metal pieces were put on a tray and the victim looked more like a normal victim of murder.

'I know some people get upset with our politicians, but somebody's taken this a step further,' Kate said.

'Kenneth Smith, MSP for Edinburgh South, I think,' Miller said. 'Currently Justice Minister tipped to be the new leader of our country.'

'Aye, he was a rising star, right enough,' Harry agreed.

'Until somebody snuffed his life out,' Lillian said. 'And this seemed to be personal. I wonder why somebody chose to end his life this way?'

'Who knows what goes through a killer's mind. Hopefully, we'll get the chance to ask him soon.'

'What about next of kin?' Miller asked.

'Charlie's finished at the doctor's. I've asked him and Elvis to go and speak to the wife. Before the press gets wind of it. This is going to be a shitstorm.'

'There's no visible sign that he was attacked

before the plates were screwed on,' Kate said. 'Let's open him up.'

Harry felt Lillian's hand on his back. He hoped she had a bucket close by. He closed his eyes as Kate made the first cut.

THIRTEEN

Charlie Skellett stood on the pavement outside the orthopaedic building on Lauriston Place, wishing he'd stayed inside. Then he saw Elvis coming along in the pool car and watched as the young DC pulled up beside him.

'That was a long five minutes, son, if you don't mind me saying so,' Skellett said, dropping himself into the passenger seat.

'I do actually. Driving through the city centre nowadays isn't exactly a fun game.'

Skellett was fiddling around with the heater controls. 'How in the name of Christ is this bastarding car freezing? You just put that heat on a minute ago, didn't you? It's not been on for long.'

'Not true,' Elvis said, booting it away from the

side of the road before a bus got near him. 'I was sweating, so I lowered it and rolled the windows down.'

'The windows down, ya wee bastard? I'm freezing my bollocks off waiting for you and then I come in here. My fridge is warmer than this.'

'This car heats up great. You'll be down to your Ys in a minute, it'll be that hot.'

'Coldest December in twelve years, that bloke on the TV said this morning. Not since that Beast from the East hit has it been so cold. Yet here you are, driving about with the windows down. Is that to stop you licking them?'

Elvis laughed as he turned left at Tollcross to head through the Meadows and up to the Grange.

'Where's Calvin this morning?' Skellett asked.

'He went through to Glasgow. His old boss got stabbed.'

'Fuck me. Is he okay?'

'He'll live. A guy dressed as Santa Claus knifed him.'

'Oh yeah, Santa Con. That's a nightmare.'

On the way to the Grange, Elvis filled Skellett in on what had gone down at the crime scene in the big house.

'How is his wife going to handle seeing him like that when she has to identify him?' Elvis asked.

'She's not. Kenneth Smith's a public figure. Harry McNeil positively identified him.'

'That's something.'

'Uniforms were sent round earlier, one of them a family liaison officer, but you know how word leaks out about this stuff. Just keep an eye out for any press, Elvis,' Skellett said as they turned into the street they were looking for: Cluny Terrace in Morningside.

'Politics pays well, I see,' Elvis said.

'That's a bit of a jaded view, son,' Skellett said.

'Aye, well, remember some of the jakeys we saw when we were stationed down in Leith? This is the opposite end of the scale.'

'Smith was a solicitor before going into politics, and you know they have a few shillings to rub together.'

'Do you talk like you're from the nineteen sixties because you wish you could travel back in time and enjoy your early manhood again?'

'Cheeky bastard. I was a bairn in the sixties.'

'If you say so,' Elvis said, grinning.

'Aw, shite,' Skellett said, seeing the vans and the

cars and the group of people who looked like they were protesting about something.

'Press,' Elvis said, making a face.

Skellett was glad to see that reinforcements had appeared and tape had been strung across the street, tied to a polis van.

'Park behind the van, keep your heid down and walk fast,' Skellett said. 'Say fuck all.'

'You mean you want me to say the words "fuck all", or say nothing?' Elvis said.

'You know what I mean.'

'I do. I just wanted you to remind me of what I already knew.'

'Nobody likes a smartarse, son.'

They got out of the car and were trying to sidle up the side of the police van, as much as a man with a walking stick can sidle, but a female reporter who recognised Skellett rushed over to him.

'Charlie, darlin',' she said, smiling and thrusting a small tape recorder out in front of her. 'Got a word for me?'

'I've got two and the second one is "off". Fill in the blank.'

'You don't mean that, love. I mean, I left your name out of the paper that time I covered corruption in the force.'

'You're hilarious.'

A uniform came walking up to them as they ducked under the tape, which was more of a circus act for Skellett, but he managed it with Elvis's help.

'Try and keep them under a bit more control, son,' Skellett said to the young man. 'Call for more help. The bloody news vans with the satellite dishes will be here soon, no doubt.'

'It's all over Twitter and Facebook,' the uniform said, following them to the driveway of the house.

'I don't care if it's all over...what's that site where men go to cheat on their girlfriends?' Skellett asked Elvis.

'How would I know?'

'*You* would know, then,' Skellett said, changing direction, eyeing up the young uniform as they walked.

'I'm married. I don't know those sites either.'

'You get my point. Get more woolly suits here, pronto.'

The uniform's eyebrows squared up to each other in between his eyes; clearly he was wondering what the older detective was talking about.

'It's what they called the guys who wore the old uniform,' Skellett explained, tutting and shaking his head.

'I never knew that either,' Elvis said as the uniform walked away.

'How would you not know about those internet places? You're supposed to be young and in the know.' Skellett knocked on the front door.

'Aye, but I'm not a perv or a granny chaser.'

'Kids nowadays,' Skellett said as the door was answered.

The FLO opened the door and the two detectives shot into the house amid a flurry of shouts and photographs being taken.

Skellett blew out a breath as the young woman closed the front door behind them.

'It's mental, sir. I've got the blinds shut, but we caught one of them in the back garden.'

'Aye, well, unless he's there to clean the windows, tell him to bog off or we'll lift him for trespassing or something. I don't suppose Mrs Smith's got a big dug?'

The FLO shook her head. 'I'm afraid not.'

'Pity. You can never find a Rottweiler when you need one. Except my wife when she's dropped one of her curlers. Right, where is she?'

'Through in the family room in the back.'

They trooped through to the room where the widow of Kenneth Smith was sitting. She'd been crying, but she'd got it under control, perhaps with the glass of red that she had balanced on the arm of the overstuffed chair.

'Mrs Smith, this is DI Skellett, and DC Presley. They're here to talk to you about your husband.'

Janet Smith looked older than she had in the photos Skellett had seen of her in the newspapers, standing next to her late husband. Maybe the crying had puffed her face up a bit, around the eyes, which were red and would probably be even redder when she sobered up. Not that she was pished, but the wine bottle was half tanned and Skellett guessed the rest would follow later on.

'Grab a pew,' she said. 'You can call me Jan. Everybody does. People I know, and since you're here to talk about Kenny, I would say that we're at least acquaintances, if not exactly on each other's Christmas card list.'

She was either very good at masking her drunkenness or this was indeed her first glass. Skellett wondered if wine lasted in the bottle after it had been opened. He wasn't sure, but maybe Elvis would know, being the wino out of the two of them.

'Okay, Jan,' he said, sitting down on an equally overstuffed settee. Elvis sat down next to him with a bounciness that made the younger detective lean towards him, so Skellett shot him a look and a silent promise of a punch in the nuts if he didn't scoot over. Elvis obliged.

'Where did you find him?' Jan asked, taking a sip of the red, and she looked over the rim of the glass as if locking eyes for battle.

'He was found in a house that was for sale on Lanark Road West. Do you know anybody who lives up that way?'

The glass was back on the arm of the chair. 'No.'

'Have you ever heard of the name Tom Powers?' Skellett asked and nodded to the FLO to sit down and stop making the place look untidy.

'No. How did the name come up, if you don't mind me asking?' Jan said.

'It just came up in the course of our enquiries,' Skellett answered.

'Oh, come on, Inspector; my husband was the Justice Minister.'

He wasn't a fucking copper, though, was he? Skellett fought the urge to throw that one in her face but carried on. Too many careers were ruined by something being misconstrued, but there was no mistaking that answer, and the police board would have no problem having him booted off the force.

'I'm afraid I can't divulge that information,' he

replied instead. 'I'm sure your husband would have understood.'

'Yes, you're right, he would have. I'm sorry for asking. I know that you'll have to rule me out as a suspect. I can give you an alibi if you give me a timeframe.'

'That's still to be determined by the pathologist, but can you tell me when you last saw him?'

Another quick sip of wine, and Skellett briefly wondered if the FLO had done much, if anything at all, to guide the woman towards a cup of tea and a packet of Hobnobs instead of a bottle.

'A few days ago. We have a mews house in Comely Bank. He's writing his memoirs, part one, so he goes there for peace sometimes. He wanted to get it finished soon as he has a deadline.'

'Who else knows you have a flat?' Skellett asked.

'Nobody. It's in my name. My maiden name. We just wanted a small place where Kenny could go and work.'

'Where is it?'

'Comely Bank.' She gave her precariously balanced wine glass a quick look before leaning over to the other side and picking up a pad and pen and scribbling the address down. Then she grabbed something else from the side table. The FLO stood up and took it from her, along with the address, and passed both to Skellett, who gave her a nod.

'That's the key for the other house. You'll be wanting to have a look round it, no doubt.'

'Thank you. We will.'

'And now you're going to ask me about enemies,' she said, her hand back to firmly grasping the glass.

'Did he have any that you know of?' Elvis asked.

Jan looked at him. 'He was in politics. Most of his enemies came from within. Back-stabbing bastards. Jealousy, that's what they felt.'

'Where is his constituency?' Skellett asked.

'Orkney. Where he came from.'

'Are you from there?'

'God, no. I've been once. Saw all there was to see and never went back.'

'I'd read about Mr Smith writing his autobiography. He got a large advance for it, didn't he?' Skellett said.

Jan nodded before putting the glass to her lips. 'Yes. A very large sum. It paid for the mews house in Comely Bank. I'll have to sell it now.'

'Did any of his constituents ever threaten him?' Skellett asked.

'No. Kenny was the golden boy in Orkney. Everybody loved him.'

'Does he still have family living there?'

Jan nodded. 'His mum and dad.'

'If you give their details to the officer there, she'll make the phone call to them.'

Jan sat quietly for a moment. 'Okay.'

'Do you have any children?' Elvis asked.

'No. Kenny didn't want any.' Her eyes had a faraway look for a moment, as if she were picturing children running around, a family that she had yearned for but never got.

'I'm going to ask you to be careful when you step outside the house,' Skellett said. 'There's press everywhere.'

'I will. I'll have a funeral director come to the house.'

Skellett stood up, followed by Elvis. 'We'll have an officer with you twenty-four hours a day until after the funeral.'

'Thank you.' Janet Smith didn't get up from her chair as the detectives left the house.

FOURTEEN

Calvin Stewart was sitting in the Incident room when the door opened and in walked someone he hadn't seen in a long time. He smiled at her and stood up.

'Wow. Bobby Dazzler! What are you doing here?' he asked her.

'I haven't heard that nickname in a long time. I could ask you the same question.'

Stewart looked around the room. 'Everybody, this is DCI Angie Fisher.'

She gave a brief nod in a general direction.

Robbie Evans was sitting next to Dunbar at a computer and nudged him. 'See? Some of them have nicknames.'

'Shut your hole.'

'So, what are you doing here?' Stewart asked Angie again.

'They wanted a senior officer for the stabbing of Davie Ross. An outside officer.' She was shorter than Stewart, coming in at around five-six, with blonde hair pulled back into a ponytail. She had on black jeans, boots and a black overcoat. All she needed was a skinhead and a neck tattoo. 'I heard that you'd been posted through to Edinburgh.'

'I am. I'd just come through when I heard about Davie,' Stewart said.

'I was briefed that he'll make it, thank God.'

'You want a coffee?'

'Sure.'

'O'Connor!'

Hamish whipped his head up from his keyboard.

'The coffee isn't going to make itself, son.'

'Oh, right. I'll put the kettle on.'

Stewart looked at Evans. 'Go and make sure the speccy bastard doesn't gob in mine.'

Evans nodded and walked over to the rickety table at the back of the room that they called their coffee station.

'Jimmy, you remember Angie, don't you?'

'Aye, of course.' Dunbar came across and shook her hand. 'How's life in Motherwell?'

115

'Can't complain. It's a wee bit quieter out there, but we still get to see some action.'

Lisa McDonald came over and Stewart introduced her. 'Nice to meet you, ma'am.'

'It's Angie. Likewise.'

'It's no' "Angie" to the redhead, Angie,' Stewart said. 'He's just dipping his toes into MIT. If your coffee tastes like pish, it's his fault.'

Hamish brought the cup over and handed it to Angie. She took a sip and smiled. 'Thanks.' She looked around the Incident room for a spare chair.

'There's a desk there. Take the weight off,' Dunbar said.

She sat down with her coffee. 'How's things coming along?'

'We got CCTV from the pub,' Lisa said. 'We see Santa bump into Davie and exchange words with him. Then we see him leave a few minutes after Davie and Joan.'

Angie nodded. 'Did anybody get anything from any other camera?' she asked.

'We did,' Hamish said, sitting back down. 'We can see Davie and Joan going down the alleyway, then Santa following them. Santa runs out the way they went in, but Davie –'

'DCS Ross to you,' Stewart growled.

'DCS Ross smacked the attacker in the knee with a bottle, so we see Santa limping as he comes back out. Which makes him easier to pick out. He gets into a taxi two streets up from the crime scene.'

'Any numbers from the taxi?' Angie asked.

'Nothing yet. We're still seeing if there are other cameras near that point,' Lisa said.

'Right, keep at it,' Angie said. Then to Stewart: 'A word in private.'

They walked back to Dunbar's office, Angie carrying her mug, and she shut the door behind her as Stewart settled into Dunbar's chair.

'Listen, Angie, if it's about me slagging off that wee ginger bastard, he got wired into me before he realised I was back from retirement. I'm going to give him a hard time for a wee while, then see how he performs.'

'You don't have to explain to me. You're the senior officer.'

'Aye, I know that, but you always lectured me. I'm sure we were married in another life.'

'I've got more things to worry about than you giving a young DC a tongue-lashing, Calvin.' She sat down opposite him.

'Oh, aye. How is the other half?'

'He found himself a little waitress. They're in London now. God rest his soul.'

'He died?' Stewart said.

'No, but I'll kill the bastard if I ever see him again. He took one of my *Simply Red* CDs. I could buy a new one, but that's not the point. I can imagine him being on top of that wee hoor with "A New Flame" playing in the background. Ironic, eh?'

Stewart saw Angie's cheeks getting redder and knew the signs. 'Imminent launch' would be the best way to describe what was going on. He'd seen it with her many times in interview rooms in the past. Some lippy bastard spewing off sexist comments about how he didn't want a 'wee lassie' interviewing him, and God forbid they should raise a hand to her. She went to kickboxing back in the day, and Stewart didn't want to risk asking her if ripping a man's nuts off was still her preferred sport.

'Aye, that was a shocker hearing about Davie,' he said, diverting attention away from Angie's ex-husband.

'It was that. Such a good boss. You know the fucker's going to pay for doing that.'

Mother of Christ. 'As much as I side with your sentiment, I'd rather see him spend a lot of time with the kiddy-fiddlers inside. We could put in a word that he's a paedo but we just couldn't prove it. Some of the boys in there will show him what a stabbing is all about.'

'Way ahead of you, boss. Listen, I spoke to Joan Devine before I came here. The assistant chief who put me on this said I should go to see Davie at the hospital first, and I did, but he was still drugged up. Poor bastard. But Lynn McKenzie was there. She's nice. You're both well-suited.'

'Aw, Christ, is there anybody who *doesn't* know about us?'

'Not many. But she's nice. I like her.'

'She's going to stay at my place in Edinburgh. We stay over at each other's place at the weekends. I'm going to stay at hers. There's a credible threat against her. Santa told Davie that Lynn's next. I won't stand by and let anybody harm her.'

'I know. I'm right there with you on that front. If we catch up with him – and I fully expect to – and he pulls a knife on me, I'm going to cut his dick off, you know that, right?'

'I wouldn't expect anything less from you, Angie.' A shiver went up Stewart's neck as he tried not to picture that scenario.

'Right. I'll go and have a walk down to where it happened. I want to see the place for myself. Then we can catch up with the uniforms doing the search for more cameras.'

'Fine by me.'

'Have you had somebody check the till receipts at the pub? See if anybody paid by card so we can trace them?' Angie asked.

'We looked at the CCTV, and when we saw who'd bumped into Davie, we checked the footage to see if he used a card. He didn't. He paid with cash.'

'The bastard knew what he was doing.'

'You and I can go down there and have a look around.'

'Great. But mind, the Assistant Chief Constable said I'm the SIO. You can tag along.'

Stewart was about to say something but thought better of it. 'Fuck me. This stabbing makes my blood boil.'

'I know it does, and if we get the guy, you'd want to stamp all over his bollocks.'

'Fucking right I would.'

'That's why they sent me in to lead the investigation.'

Stewart looked away for a second, picturing his boot firmly planted round the guy's bollocks, and then nodded his head and looked Angie in the eyes. 'I know you'll do a good job.'

'I will. You have to trust me.'

'If I've ever trusted anybody in this job, it's you.'

Angie stood up. 'Good. Keep those happy thoughts.'

They left the office and found Robbie Evans talking football with Hamish.

'Right, if you two fucking sweetie wives can tear yourselves away from each other for just a minute, pay attention. I'm going to the pub with DCI Fisher. To have a talk with the owner about Davie Ross, before you think we're going for a sesh,' Stewart said. 'Jimmy? Evans? Go and make contact with uniforms, see if they've had any luck with the CCTV search.'

'Right you are, sir,' Evans replied.

'We're away to find an old man's club so we can sit and play dominoes for the rest of the day. Isn't that right, Ginge?'

'Whatever you say, sir.'

'Poor guy,' Angie said. 'I bet he's going to be glad when you go back to Edinburgh.'

'Feel free to take him back to Motherwell with you. I'm sure he'll be pleased to see *you* so he won't have to see me again.'

She smiled and looked at Stewart. 'Nobody's pleased to see me, except when I leave the room.

They all want to see my arse being banged by the door as I leave.'

Evans looked at her. 'I'm sure that's not right, ma'am.'

Angie grinned. 'The boy doesn't know me yet, Calvin.'

'He's a slow learner. He'll get the picture soon enough.'

'I think I've just been insulted,' Evans said to Dunbar as they followed Angie out of the Incident room, watching the door to see if it would hit her on the arse, but she was too quick.

FIFTEEN

It was late afternoon by the time Harry got down to Comely Bank and the mews house where Kenneth Smith had been writing his memoirs.

He and Miller stood in the quiet street, not far from Harry's old flat. Lillian O'Shea had the key in her hand, Elvis close behind.

Skellett had said he needed some painkillers and to rest his leg, so he was back in the Incident room.

There were three terraced houses here, each of them with a garage. They had been carriage houses back in the day, like so many mews homes.

'Nice place,' Lillian said. She too lived just round the corner, but in a flat, like Harry's.

'You can put in an offer,' Elvis said. 'Mrs Smith is going to be putting it on the market.'

'Really? I would have thought she would want to keep a place like this.'

'Mr Smith got an advance from the publisher, but they'll want it back. This place was bought under her maiden name.'

'I would have thought the insurance pay-out would pay for this place,' Harry said.

'Charlie's working on that just now. To see who benefits and by how much.'

'Aye, well, we all know how many spouses have been murdered for the insurance pay-out.' Harry looked at the outside of the house; the curtains had been drawn. 'Let's get a move on; I'm bloody freezing out here.'

Lillian stepped forward with the key and opened the front door. She hit the light switch and they walked in. A kitchen was on the left. No dishes were out and the counters were clear except for a toaster and a kettle.

On the other side was a small living room. A couch and TV, with nothing else.

Harry walked forward, the others behind him in the narrow hallway. There was a small bathroom just ahead and beyond an open door on the right was a bedroom.

The door on the left was closed.

'Right, son, get that door open,' Harry said to Elvis.

The young detective stepped forward, keenly aware he may be the front line of defence against a nutcase who had a penchant for screwing metal plates into corpses. He turned the handle and shoved the door hard enough to almost rip it off the hinges.

Another bedroom.

'Right, let's get up these stairs and see what's up there,' Harry said. Miller and Elvis looked at him.

'After you, I meant. No point in having a dog and barking yourself.' Harry put a hand on Elvis's shoulder and guided him towards the narrow staircase. It was carpeted and didn't squeak, but he was sure the fact that they had been talking and banging about would have given the killer a heads-up.

Halfway up the stairs, Elvis stopped to turn and look at them. 'If I see somebody with an electric drill and a carving knife, I'll be sure to let you know so you can effect an escape.'

'That's the spirit,' Harry said.

Elvis tutted and made his way to the top and turned onto a landing. They heard him bump along the hallway above and open a door, and they knew it was a good sign when he didn't scream.

There wasn't one, but they heard Elvis shout

instead. Not screams of agony, and nor were there any sounds of a fight going on. What they did hear was a quick 'Fuck me' before Elvis shouted, 'You need to come up here and see this.'

Harry made his way up, with Miller and Lillian following. They saw Elvis standing in an open doorway.

'There's a desk with a computer on it through in there,' he said, pointing to a closed door.

The door was partly open and they could see that Elvis had put the light on. He pushed the door wider and then they all saw where Kenneth Smith had died.

'Let's get Callum Craig and his team in here,' Harry said, and they all shuffled out, like tourists who were exploring an old castle. Not allowed to touch anything and careful to move in an orderly fashion.

Then Harry opened the bathroom door, and this was a whole new ballgame.

SIXTEEN

The Brass Monkey bar was tucked away in Springfield Court, a lane off Buchanan Street. The light was saying cheerio for the day, replaced by the neon and Christmas lights draped all over the place.

'Thank Christ they're not playing Christmas music,' Angie said as she and Stewart walked along the narrow alleyway. A doorman was standing in front of the short flight of steps leading to the bar entrance. He was young, with a shaved head, and looked like he had thought the only time he would ever be wearing a suit in his lifetime was when they were screwing the lid down. But somebody had made him wear one in order to stand in front of this door.

'I'm here to see Mick Spencer, your manager,' Angie said, while Stewart stood back.

'Are you now, sweetheart?' the bouncer said, looking disinterested. 'You don't look like his usual type. Bit old for him.' He smiled.

'Get out my fucking way, ya gormless bastard,' she said.

His smile dropped. 'Look, why don't you fuck off and come back when we're less busy.'

Stewart winced, like he had just given himself a paper cut. Maybe the bouncer had a paper cut and that was why he was in such a bad mood, but Stewart knew the younger man was going to be in a world of pain very shortly. There *was* a reason Angie had been posted to Motherwell, after all.

'I think we'll just go in now. Step aside.'

The bouncer made the nearly fatal mistake of almost touching Angie. He put out a hand, trying to shove her away. For a woman in her forties, she was quick. She grabbed his wrist and twisted it, then reached down and grabbed his bollocks.

He let out a yell and tried to bend, following the direction his arm had suddenly taken, but the gloved hand that was grabbing his balls prevented that.

'Listen to me, fuck face. My name is DCI Angie Fisher. Memorise it. Write it down on a piece of paper and stick it on your fridge with a magnet if you have to. But whatever you do, you'd better learn to spell it. Because if you and I ever cross paths again, I'll tell my superiors that you assaulted me, resulting in your death. There will be an enquiry, of course, but I have friends everywhere. Friends who will back me up to the hilt. Pardon the pun.'

More pressure on his balls. More attempts at squealing like a wee lassie but finding he didn't have enough air to let one go.

'I will stick a knife right through your cock before I slice your femoral artery and you'll bleed out where you fall.' One more tight squeeze. 'Do you understand me?'

'Yes.' It was an answer given in a low tone that an old man might use after he'd struggled up a hill for a bus and only had enough breath left to chastise the driver with a short, "Where the fuck have you been?"

'I can't hear you,' Angie said, leaning in closer.

The bouncer made eye contact with Stewart, who was standing there with a bemused look. The bouncer was silently pleading for help but none was forthcoming.

'Yes.' The bouncer said it louder, and Stewart could swear he saw tears in his eyes.

'Now, you're not going to start throwing threats

at me when I let you go, are you? Like, you'll find me and do me in. Or have your friends come look for me. Because I'll fuck them over just before I come looking for you.'

'No.' A barely heard whisper again.

Then another suit appeared with two mugs of coffee. 'Gregor, ya fucking eejit. Don't you know who that is?'

Gregor gently shook his head, looking like he was going to faint at any minute.

'That's DCI Fisher.' The new guy nodded to her. 'And my good friend Superintendent Stewart. How are you both?'

'Just fine,' Angie said. 'I was just playing a little game of "see who's going to blink first" and I think I won.'

'It's true,' Stewart said, digging his hands deeper into his pockets. 'She won. Now can we come in and speak to your boss?'

'Of course you can. As soon as this young lady finishes with Gregor's bollocks.'

Angie smiled and let go of Gregor's balls and arm. The bouncer's face had found no reason to keep any colour in it and had changed to white. Whatever rosy cheeks he'd had from standing out in the cold were now gone.

'I need to use the bathroom,' he said, climbing the short flight of steps into the pub proper.

'Daft laddie. I knew he was going to be trouble. And the one he picks it with is Angie Fisher. He's a fucking clown.' The older man took a sip of his coffee. 'In you go. It's freezing out here.'

'Thanks, Stan,' Stewart said.

'Good seeing you again, Stan,' Angie said. 'Life treating you well?'

'It is. The daughter's getting married next summer. I'm trying to lose a few pounds to fit into a tux.'

'Just wear your bouncer's suit,' Stewart said. 'You'll be fine.'

'If I do that, some bastard will have me standing at the door.' Stan put the two mugs down. 'You want me to radio ahead or do you want to surprise him?'

'Let's go with the surprise,' Angie said.

'As you wish. He's in his office, counting his pennies.'

They walked into the pub and through a back corridor, no sign of Gregor anywhere, and Angie knocked on the manager's door.

'Stan, for fuck's sake, I'm busy.'

Angie knocked again. 'Police. We need a word.'

She didn't wait for an invite but opened the door and walked in.

'Jesus,' the owner of the bar said. A fat, balding man called Aaron Ruff. 'What if I'd been standing in my skids just now?'

'I've never known you to be shy, Aaron,' Stewart said.

'Oh, Mr Stewart. Didn't see it was you,' Ruff said. 'Do you know how long those white suits were here going over every inch of my bar?'

'No, but if you hum it...' Angie said.

Ruff tutted. 'They've cost me a fortune. Finger-printing the place. There was more white powder in here than...' He stopped suddenly.

'Than what?' Angie said. She and Stewart stood looking at Ruff over his desk.

'Than a baker's workbench,' he said lamely. 'Do you want to take a seat?'

There was one hard chair sitting on its own against a wall, and Ruff looked at them as if this was the last chance at winning musical chairs, but neither detective moved.

'We were wondering if you've heard anything regarding our boss being stabbed, Aaron?' Stewart said.

'Me? No. You know I would be calling you if I heard anything, Mr Stewart.'

'Fuck me, are we going to do this dance every time we meet now? I mean, Stan out there is much more sociable than you are these days.'

'Stan? What did he tell you?'

'Something very interesting,' Angie said.

'Aw, for God's sake. But you know something? That booze was for a private party. He knows that. I mean, Customs doesn't need to get involved. That would make my life hell, and for what? You know I'm straight as an arrow when it comes to my bars.'

'Christ, you didn't want to get Customs involved? Oh, no. I didn't know that,' Angie said. 'Oops. And now I can't remember their phone number, or else I'd call back and tell them I've made a mistake.'

'Aw, away. Please tell me you haven't? Please, Mr Stewart. I've got kids to feed.'

'You have two Rottweilers,' Stewart said.

'They're my kids.'

'Maybe a good shelter will take them when you're inside.'

'Oh, no, please don't talk like that. My mother's ill. I'm trying to find enough money to send her to the States for life-saving treatment. You wouldn't begrudge a son doing that for his mother, would you?'

'I thought your mother was deid?' Stewart said.

'That's my adopted mother. I'm talking about my biological mother.'

'I need to know if any of your regulars knew the guy who was in here last night and bumped into Davie Ross.'

'God, that's piss poor, somebody doing that to him.'

'That's fine, Aaron, skirt around the subject all you like, but your mother will be lucky if she has enough money left to catch a bus to see you in the Bar L. Because let's face it, that's the only bar you'll be inside when Customs are finished with you. They'll be crawling so far up your arse with a microscope, they'll be able to remove any polyps while they're at it.'

'That's disgusting, even for you, if I may say so.'

'Fine,' Angie said. 'Keep dodging the question, but Customs don't give a fuck at the end of the day. If they don't think they have enough evidence on you, they'll just add shit to it to make anything stick. They're a law unto themselves.'

'You know, if they made a TV show starring you two, you'd be called "Rock" and "Hard Place", because that's where I am right now, between a rock and a hard place.'

'I understand that you think your clients will think you're a snitch, and that's fine. Maybe they'll all club together to buy your mother a bus pass. Because she'll be needing one, she'll be visiting you that often.'

'Alright, but you didn't hear it from me, okay?' Ruff looked between the two detectives. 'Please? It's hard enough getting the punters in with the way prices of everything have gone through the roof. If they think they're being spied on, the next time you come in here, there'll be tumbleweed blowing about. A skeleton would be sitting at the piano if we had one. I'm not kidding either.'

'Spare us the sob story, Aaron. Do you know who he is or not?'

'Okay. He's not one of my regulars. But he was chatting to other Santa's while he was having a beer. Before he bumped into Davie. I was helping out behind the bar. Aye, I know, eh? Aaron Ruff getting his hands dirty. But it's true. Sometimes I get behind the bar. I like to keep my hand in. Said the retired gynaecologist. But anyway, it seemed like one of the other Santa's knew him. It was hard to tell, because they just pulled their fake beards down so they could drink. I don't know who this bloke was, but the one you're after said his name was Eddie Bartlett.'

'There you go, Aaron,' Angie said. 'Don't think of it as grassing, think of it as your civic duty.'

'Well, I just hope he doesn't come back and stick me like he did Davie Ross.'

SEVENTEEN

The victim was a redhead. He looked to be in his forties, and the rictus of pain that was stamped on his face when he died remained.

Like Kenny Smith, he had metal plates screwed into him to hold him in place on the metal stand under his feet. They too were screwed in. His hands were out in front of him, like he was strangling fresh air. He was dressed in a shirt and trousers but no shoes or socks.

'Christ Almighty,' Lillian said. 'Two of them. With another mannequin in the bath water.'

Harry nodded and stayed where he was as Callum Craig came into the house, the door having been opened by Elvis. There was a crew with Craig, all suited up ready to go into action. He was the first one up the stairs.

'What have we got, Harry?' the younger man asked.

'Take a look for yourself, son.' Harry stepped out onto the landing.

'Jesus. Just like the one this morning,' Craig said.

'Exactly,' Lillian said. 'It looks like maybe soap has been added to the water to cloud it.'

'It looks like acid, but it's obviously not or the mannequin would be melted,' Harry said from behind.

'I'll get it photographed and we'll do our stuff in here.'

'Before you go back downstairs, have a look in there,' Harry said, pointing to the bedroom.

Craig came out of the bathroom and approached the bedroom with its dull light.

'Jesus. This is a new one on me,' Craig said.

There were pieces of metal and screws strewn about the floor and on a wooden dining table, littering the room. But it was the blood spatter on the wallpaper that caught his attention. And small pieces of skin. The carpet hadn't fared any better and had got the drill aftermath treatment.

'Looks like Santa's workshop exploded and took

some elves with it,' Craig said.

'That's Christmas ruined for me,' Lillian said. 'Bloody exploding elves.'

'At least they didn't explode in *your* house,' Harry said. Christmas was a couple of weeks away and he'd been twisting his brain trying to think of what he could get for Alex. What did you get for a wife you'd thought was dead for almost a year and who then came back into your life? A padlock and chain? A tracker? Things were getting easier, but they had a way to go yet.

'Do you think he's finished?' Craig asked. 'Our killer?'

'Who knows?'

Craig went to speak to his crew.

Harry entered the room again. 'This house belonged to Kenny Smith, even though it was in his wife's name. He may or may not have been killed here, along with our friend in the bathroom. Unless the guy through there was the one who was killed here and bolted together. The simple answer is, we don't know.'

'We'll be able to tell from the samples we take if Smith was killed here,' Craig said. 'It's going to take a little bit of time, though.'

'The first dummy had blood on it, but this one

doesn't,' Lillian said, coming in behind him.

'Look at the way his hands are positioned,' Harry said. 'It's like he was strangling her. The first one had paint on it to simulate blood, like he had stabbed her.'

'I don't recognise this man, boss, do you?' Lillian said.

Harry shook his head. 'Not this time. We can work on the assumption that he knew Smith, unless we find out otherwise. Callum there can get us fingerprints, see if he's in the system. There's nothing on him to identify him. Maybe Smith's widow can shine a light on who he is. But let's move away and let the team get going on this.'

Harry and Lillian walked down the stairs to the hallway, where Elvis was talking to a young woman in a white suit. She nodded and then left.

'That room is where Smith was working on his memoirs,' he explained. 'There are papers on the desk in the corner, and a laptop is sitting there, closed. I've asked the tech to get it printed, then we can have our computer guys look at it.'

'Good job,' Harry said. 'Get uniforms to seal off this street. They're going to be hours at it yet. One of the pathologists will have to come out and have a look.' He looked at his watch. 'Meantime, go and get something to eat.'

EIGHTEEN

The flat felt empty without Stewart being there. Lynn McKenzie had tossed her overnight bag onto the bed and opened a bottle of wine. She already had clothes here, but there were other things to bring.

She sat down at the small table at the front window but kept the curtains closed. Calvin was worrying like a mother hen: don't stand close to the window, make sure the door's locked, have Harry McNeil's number on speed dial.

She looked at her phone and went to Harry's name in her contact list. She tapped the number and listened to it ringing. And ringing. She was about to hang up when he answered.

'Harry, it's Lynn McKenzie. I was just letting you know I'm at Calvin's flat in Comely Bank. He told me to call you and let you know when I was settled in.'

'*That's fine, ma'am. If you need me for anything, just give me a shout. I'm actually just round the corner at a crime scene. Do you need me for anything just now?*'

'I don't want to drag you away from anything.'

'*We're pulling out now to let forensics get to grips with the place. It's a similar murder to the one we had this morning.*'

'Okay then, if you fancy coming up for a quick coffee, you can fill me in and I can report it to Calvin.'

'*I'm literally five minutes away. Just round the corner.*'

'I'll get the kettle on.' She hung up and went through to the kitchen and poured fresh water into the kettle before turning it on. It hadn't even boiled by the time she heard the knock on the door.

'Harry, come in,' she said. 'I bought a fish supper. If I'd known I was going to have company, I would have bought two.'

'That's fine, ma'am. I'll be heading home for dinner in a little while.'

'Harry, we're in the flat that you own. You can call me Lynn.'

Harry felt a bit awkward for a second, then nodded. 'Lynn it is.'

'I just heard the kettle click off. Come on through and we can have a coffee. Although I poured myself a wine too, just to take the edge off.'

'The threat is credible. I'd need a glass of wine too.'

They went through to his kitchen, but he didn't think of it as *his* kitchen anymore. He'd been here with Alex, and had found her collapsed here, and any happy memories it held were long gone.

They worked as a team: coffee jar, pour water, add milk. They each grabbed their own mug and took it through to the living room and sat down.

'How are things with you and Alex?' she asked, leaving the coffee alone and having a sip of the wine.

Harry nodded. 'Things are good. We're still working on it, but Alex keeps beating herself up over the fact that she was away from Grace for nearly a year, even though it was to keep our daughter safe. She thinks that Grace won't bond with her and will think Alex's sister, Jessica, is her mother.'

'Jessica still stays with you, doesn't she?'

'Yes. It's a big house with plenty of room for all of us, and she wants to be a support system for Alex, and she's fantastic. She tells Alex that Grace won't even remember all of this when she's older.'

Lynn ate some chips and broke the fish in half. 'Here, get wired in. You must be starving.'

'I have to admit, it smells fantastic. Thanks.'

'I appreciate you letting me stay here,' she said, the aroma of the brown sauce better than perfume.

'Calvin rents it; it's his place. It wasn't up to me, but it wouldn't have been a problem if it had been.'

'Still, you're the landlord. Calvin really does appreciate you giving him a good deal. He thinks highly of you, Harry.'

'And me of him.' He ate the fish, not realising he had been so hungry. He noticed the TV was off and wondered if he had spoiled her viewing time.

'I think people will wonder how Calvin and I got together,' she said.

'It's nobody's business,' Harry replied after he'd washed the fish down.

'I know, but people talk. They see me as a timid super who got to her position because she's a woman.'

'Lynn, there are plenty of female officers who go high up.'

'It's getting better, I have to admit, but now here I am, sleeping with another superintendent. There are people who think Calvin should have stayed retired, and if they knew about me and him, they would think I need my head examined. I know he can be uncouth and he uses language that my grandmother would have fainted over, but deep inside he's a caring man who loves his daughter and grandson. And he cares about me. I see a different side to him.'

It was as if she had got Harry up here to explain her relationship with Stewart, but there was no need. Each to their own.

'I'm glad things are working out for you.'

'Thank you, Harry. Let's finish this fish supper and I'll let you get off home to Alex.'

'I can stay a while longer. Then when I go, I'll have a uniform posted downstairs.'

She smiled at him. 'You'll go a long way, Harry McNeil.'

NINETEEN

DS Julie Stott stood inside the lobby of The Edinburgh Grand in St Andrew Square, soaking in the warmth. There was an outside entrance to the Lady Libertine bar in West Register Street, but it was too cold to hang about out there, so she was waiting outside the interior entrance door.

He wasn't late. She was just early. She was excited, like a schoolgirl going to the high school prom. God knows why; her first impression of him was that he was a smartarse, but he gave off a certain charm too.

People were coming and going, guests going to the lifts to go up to their rooms. People coming into the Hawksmoor restaurant. Not so many coming out of the bar.

She had her phone out, looking at the screen, pretending to be texting somebody. The male receptionist behind the counter had smiled a couple of times at her like she was some sad cow.

She looked at her watch even though the time was on her phone, making it look like her date hadn't turned up, and she was about to leave, thinking she'd made a mistake coming here, when the front doors to the hotel opened automatically and in walked the man she was waiting for.

Dan Jenkins.

He smiled at her, all confidence and hair gel, and despite herself, she smiled back. *Christ, he's here because he wants to tell you something about the case, ye mad cow,* she reminded herself.

'I'm not late, am I?' he said, knowing full well he wasn't.

'No, no, I was just skulking about in here like I'm about to go up and tan a room.'

'You're too good-looking to be one of those people.'

'Trust me, I'm a cop. It takes all sorts.'

'The only thing you would steal is a man's heart.' His smile got even wider.

Jesus, he is good, I'll give him that. She smiled

back, though, genuinely impressed. 'Shall we?' she said, and he opened the door to the bar.

They went to get the drinks. Dan suggested she sit at a table and he'd get them, but she wasn't some daft wee lassie who would let a man buy her a drink and then pop in a roofie. She watched the barman take the cap off her beer, then she didn't take her eyes off it until it was in her hand.

They found a table in a corner.

'If I was a lesser man, I would be offended that you don't trust me,' he said, the perma-grin still on his face.

'You know I'm a police officer, right? We don't trust anybody.'

'Well, here's to a new friendship.'

They clinked bottles. 'You said you had new information when you called me,' she said.

'I got to thinking about the guy who came to the house, Tom Powers. The more I think about it, the more I think his beard was fake. I think he dressed up to fool us so we couldn't identify him. It looked like one of those fake Santa beards.'

'And yet you both went back to show him round again.'

Dan sipped his cold beer. Nodded. Then put the bottle on the table. 'You wouldn't believe some of the nut jobs we deal with. And I mean the ones with money. They're eccentric, some of them. They don't want to be recognised, which is fine by me.'

Julie nodded. This wasn't the big mystery-solver she was hoping for. She'd hoped for something that she could run with, something that would lead to an arrest. She wondered if Dan had made this up just to have a drink with her.

Then she reminded herself that she had agreed to come out for a drink with him. She could have told him to meet her at the station, where he could have spewed his fairy tales, but she hadn't.

'Any luck with the case?' he asked her.

'Not really. We need to go through you and Ms Taylor's client list. Something might jump out at us. The lab is going through the fingerprints just now, to see if there's a match of any kind.'

Then she kicked herself. *You're MIT, for God's sake. You're telling a stranger, somebody who's involved in the case, how the case is going.*

'I can't go into more details, Dan.'

He sat back with his hands up. 'Oh, crap, I shouldn't have asked. I don't want to get you in trouble. It's just that I'm personally involved.'

'It's okay.' She took a drink and looked around at the other couples, having a good time. She hadn't had a boyfriend in a long time and admitted it felt good to be sitting here with a man.

'There is something else I wanted to run past you,' he said.

She looked at him, ready to shoot him down in flames. 'I'm listening.'

He sat forward again, leaving his bottle where it was. 'I know I seemed a bit cocky when you interviewed me –'

'Just a bit.'

He held up a hand again. 'But I was in the moment. You see, I'm fed up with this house-selling game. I mean, it's okay, but you have to rely on getting a sale to make money. Our wages aren't guaranteed. That's why I've been thinking of a career switch for a while.'

'And now you want to be a copper,' she said, smiling.

'Yes.'

Her smile dropped. 'Oh. You're serious?' she said.

'I am. I felt I was in the zone back in that house. I know you were the one asking the questions, but I felt we were a team, that it was you and me in there, interviewing somebody as a team. Didn't you feel that connection?'

'I was interviewing you, Dan. I'm sorry if I didn't feel the same way.'

He laughed. 'Maybe not at that moment, but I bet you thought about it afterwards. Gave *me* another thought.'

She gave a little smirk. Cocky bastard. 'Let's just say, I'm sitting here with you now, aren't I?'

'I knew it!' He laughed again. 'So, what do you say, Julie? Can you give me some tips on how to get into the police force? And of course, we could do it over dinner too, because I'm sure I'll have some follow-up questions.'

'Christ, you're persistent, aren't you?'

'I am.'

'Okay, I'm sure I could give you some tips.'

They had some more drinks and Dan surprised her when he stood up and looked at his watch. 'We don't want to be late.'

'Late for what?'

'Dinner. Or have you already eaten?'

'No, I haven't eaten.'

'I booked a table at the Hawksmoor in the hotel here.'

'You're full of surprises.'

'I aim to please. Care to join me? I mean, I'd look

like a right sad case sitting in there on my own instead of having a beautiful woman at my table.'

She laughed, the few bottles of beer loosening her up. She was starting to really like him.

'Okay, kind sir. Lead the way.'

TWENTY

Harry closed his front door and was pleased to be home. It felt like the missing piece of the puzzle had finally fallen into place when Alex came home.

'Hi, honey,' she said, coming into the hallway from the kitchen. 'How was your day?'

'Very weird. I mean, not my day, just the victims we found,' he replied, taking his coat off. He walked over to her and gave her a kiss. Sometimes he had to shake off the feeling that he was kissing an apparition.

'Jessica's away out with her friends and Grace is in bed.'

'Yeah, sorry I'm late.'

'You don't ever have to apologise. That's the job we're in. I'm a copper too, remember?'

'How's Max?' DI Max Hold, Alex's immediate boss.

'He's doing fine. I think he's getting fed up living in Anstruther and wants to move down the road a bit to Kirkcaldy.'

'Are you working on anything interesting?' Harry asked as Alex put some Chinese food onto a plate and stuck it into the microwave.

'Suspicious death. An old boy found in his bathtub by his carer. It won't set the world on fire. How about you?'

'These two deaths today.' He shook his head. 'Somebody killed them and posed them using metal brackets and plates, screwing them into their limbs.'

'Jesus, that sounds painful.'

'It was post-mortem. Finbar sent a preliminary report giving us a heads-up. You know, something about the first scene bothered me. Not the victim, although that was strange enough, but the room.'

'The room?'

'Aye. The first victim was found in a gardener's cottage by a big house for sale. The room had been staged, that was obvious. But there was something about it that I've seen recently.'

'Déjà vu?'

'Something like that.'

The microwave dinged and Alex took the plate out. 'You want to sit in here or with a TV tray in the living room?'

'The big couch is calling my name. I'm knackered. I'll eat in there. I'll just pop up and see the little lady first.'

He left the kitchen, his mind a million miles away, and went into his daughter's room quietly and saw her sleeping. He smiled and gently closed the door again, then went downstairs.

'You know what Charlie Skellett told me?' he said to Alex as he sat on the couch. 'Thanks for doing this.' He spooned a mouthful of the chicken fried rice into his mouth.

'I give up. What *did* Charlie say to you?'

'He said a *Dr Who* exhibition has opened at the museum. He's going to take his grandkids. I wondered if you wanted to go tomorrow, since you're such a big fan.'

'That sounds magic! I love *Dr Who*. We can take Grace. I'm sure she'll love it.'

'Great. That'll be nice for us to have a wee family day out. It might have to be later in the day, what with this case landing in our lap.'

She nodded. 'Or I could take Jessica if she's not doing anything. I know you'll be up to your ears in this murder.'

'Whatever you feel like.'

They watched TV while Harry ate, but the thought of the room where Kenny Smith was found wouldn't leave him. Just one little detail was hovering around in his head. Something he'd seen before. And not too long ago.

TWENTY-ONE

Visiting times were over, but not for Calvin Stewart and Angie Fisher. This was an investigation and nobody questioned them.

'Christ, I'm starving,' Angie said, trying to rock the vending machine.

'Here, you'll set the fucking alarm off,' Stewart said. 'Some poor nurse will go running, thinking an old codger's final moments have arrived, and it's only you trying to tan a free *Milky Way*.'

'Sometimes one gets stuck and it's already been paid for, so it's not stealing,' she said, grinning.

'Do you see any about to fall?' Stewart said, shaking his head. 'Deary me. You'll get us both lifted for chorying a chocolate bar. What's the world coming to? Here, let me buy one for you.' He took his credit card out and swiped it. 'Go ahead. Don't say I don't spoil you.'

She laughed and hit the button for a *Mars Bar*. 'Last of the big spenders. What would Lynn say if she knew you were buying me chocolate?' She reached in behind the flap, took the bar out and unwrapped it.

'It would depend how you worded it. Buying you chocolates and buying you a chocolate bar out of a foosty old hospital machine are two different things.'

'Don't worry, your secret's safe with me.'

'There's no secret. There's nothing to worry about.'

'I'm just pulling your plonker,' she replied. 'As it were.'

They walked towards Davie Ross's room. 'Have you moved on after the debacle with your ex-husband?' Stewart asked, wishing he'd bought himself a sweetie now.

'He's a total wanker.'

'Not quite, then.'

'You want a bite?' Angie asked, holding out the half-eaten bar. There was a string of caramel hanging off the end.

'After you've slavered all over it? I'll pass.'

She shrugged. 'Suit yourself.' Two bites and it

was gone. 'You know, I want to move on, but it's been a year and there's a trust issue there now. I've been out on a couple of dates, but then I had too much to drink and made an arse of myself.'

'Young Robbie Evans is getting married. Can you believe that?'

'To a woman?'

'Aye, to a woman,' Stewart said.

'I always thought he was...you know...'

'Gay?'

'Aye, gay.'

'He's not gay. It wouldn't have mattered if he was. I mean, his girlfriend works with a gay guy and he's a great laugh. She works with Muckle McInsh as well. You remember him?'

'Muckle? Of course I remember him. Christ, I haven't seen him for ages.'

'He's not polis anymore. He, wee Shug and Vern started a private investigations place. I retired and did some work for them.'

Angie laughed. 'If I managed to get out, I think I would stay out.'

'Aye, well, I got bored. My wee pal Finbar O'Toole did it as well. He quit being a pathologist, but he's back at that game now and he works through in Edinburgh. You'd like him. Small but hard as nails.'

'You'll have to tell me where Muckle's based so I can go and have a coffee with him.'

'His wife left him. He's just waiting on the divorce coming through. Now he's an almost-eligible bachelor again.'

'I'm doing just fine, thanks. I even gave consideration to moving to Fife.'

'But they're all daft in Fife.'

'They probably think we're all daft.'

They stopped outside Ross's room and waited while a nurse finished checking his vitals. On the other side of the doorway stood a uniform and he nodded to Stewart, recognising him.

'Evening, sir. Ma'am.'

Stewart and Angie both nodded to the man.

'Smelly fucking place this is,' Stewart said. 'I'm not going to lie, this gives me the willies, being in here with people who aren't going to make it through the night.'

'It's disinfectant, Calvin, no' dog shite.'

'I can see why Harry McNeil hates the mortuary. The hospitals are the same. Squeaky vinyl floors, machines beeping. You can almost hear the dead walking along the corridors.'

'Christ, don't go in there talking like that,' Angie said. 'You'll put the shitters right up him.'

The nurse left and smiled at them. 'You can go in,' she said, speed-walking away.

They went into Ross's room and closed the door.

'I might have been stabbed, but I'm not deef,' Ross said. He was sitting up, some machines attached to him, keeping an eye on his vitals, while one arm had a drip in it. 'Bloody ghosts. I'll no' be able to sleep now, thinking some zombie's going to come in and finish the job that arsehole started.'

'Just relax, Davie, or you'll have the heart monitor exploding,' Stewart said. 'And look who the cat dragged in.'

'Shut up,' Angie said, stepping forward and smiling at the older detective. 'Good to see you again, sir. I was shocked when I was put in charge of this case.'

'ACC Peterson put you up to this?' Ross said and winced.

'Aye, he did. He and I go way back. He doesn't give a toss that I was sent packing to Motherwell.'

'I wish that you were still at Helen Street. Have you seen the wee twats they're bringing in now?'

'I have. But just you relax, sir.'

'My side was hurting earlier, but the nurse gave

161

me something for it, and it wasn't a nip of Johnnie Walker's,' Ross said.

'Did Joan come in to see you?' Stewart asked.

'Aye. She's still here. Or did you think that coat and handbag were mine?' Ross nodded to one of the chairs. 'She went away for something to eat. I told her to look after herself.'

'Aye, well, I was going to bring you in a *Mars Bar*, but Angie ate it coming along the corridor.'

'Lying bastard,' Angie said. 'We were going to get you some flowers and a teddy bear, but the gift shop was closed.'

'I've had a wee scran. I have to just eat a wee bit or else I'll be plastering the walls.'

'Jesus, Davie, this place is honking enough without you adding to it,' Stewart said.

'Sit down, Angie,' Ross said, indicating the empty chair next to the one with the coat and bag on it.

Angie sat down, leaving Stewart to fend for himself. He leaned against the wall by the window.

'I don't suppose you've found the bastard who did this?' Ross asked.

'Aye. We picked him up in the North Pole. He tried to give us some shite that he was in a workshop or something, surrounded by a bunch of little people, but we didn't buy it.'

'You're hilarious, Calvin. So that would be a no.'

'Aye. We managed to get a name, though,' Angie said. 'Does Eddie Bartlett jump out at you?'

'Just the other night with a bloody knife.'

'We googled it after the system came up empty. There were a few results, but one that stuck out was the name of a character in a James Cagney movie.'

'Christ, that doesn't help, does it? But where did you get the name from?'

'Aaron Ruff at *The Brass Monkey*,' Angie said.

'I'd rely on a fucking nonce before I'd rely on that wee bastard.'

'Unless the guy was letting people know his name, which was fake, to send us in a different direction,' Stewart said.

'Could be. You were lucky Joan was with you,' Angie said to Ross.

'My ears are burning,' Joan said, coming back into the room. 'Somebody talking about me?'

'We are,' Ross said. 'Just saying you're a godsend.'

'Och, away. I wasn't going to let that bloody thug get another stab at my friend.'

'Boyfriend,' Stewart corrected.

'Oh, for God's sake, Calvin Stewart. Listen to you; boyfriend.'

'I think they know about us, Joan,' Ross said.

'Right. But we're too old to be called boyfriend/girlfriend.'

'Domestic partners?' Angie suggested.

'And what the bloody hell is that when it's at home?' Ross asked her.

Joan laughed. 'We'd been talking about retiring and selling up and moving somewhere warm.'

'I'm getting too old for this shite,' Ross confirmed.

'You deserve it, Davie,' Stewart said. 'Take it easy, sit around with your feet up, drink tea all day. Do sod all. Just like you do in the office.'

'Cheeky bastard. But it's time to hand over the reins. I'll be talking to somebody upstairs about it.' The other three looked at Ross in silence. 'No' the big man upstairs. Tulliallan.'

'Oh, right,' they all mumbled.

Ross looked at Joan. 'If you're still willing to come with me.'

'Of course I am, you daft bugger. I've had enough of working.'

Ross smiled and looked at Stewart. 'Listen, son, did you get anywhere with the cold case I asked you to look into?'

'The Orkney one?'

'Aye.'

'Nothing so far. I was thinking of maybe sending a couple of the team out there, but I don't know if the high heid yins would sign off on a wee trip.'

'I'll make sure it's signed off if you do decide to go with them.'

'Aye, maybe I could do with a wee hoolie right enough. I'll make sure Elvis keeps looking into it.'

Joan raised her eyebrows until Stewart told her that was the name of one of the team members and they weren't communicating with the late singer himself.

'Just let me know. After what the attacker said when I was on the ground: "You and that bitch Lynn McKenzie should have kept your fucking nose out of it." That's what he said. I know she and I have worked on cases together for a long time, but that was one that jumped out at me.'

'We'll look into it, Davie,' Angie said.

'I think we'll leave you two lovebirds to get on with it,' Stewart said. Ross and Joan looked at him. 'Well, you know what I mean. Not get *on* with it. I mean, have a bite to eat. Have a chat. Not have a go, or anything. But if you were planning on that, then fine, but I meant just –'

'Calvin, let's go and leave Davie and Joan in peace,' Angie said.

'Aye. Let's do that.'

'Take care, sir. Nice meeting you again, Joan,' Angie said.

'You too. And if Davie and I ever tie the knot, I'd like you both to be there.'

'We'd love to.'

Stewart gave an awkward wave as he and Angie left the room.

'Christ, I had a brain fart,' he said. 'I hope Joan didn't think I was being crude or anything.'

'Nobody thinks you're crude, Calvin,' Angie replied. 'Much.'

TWENTY-TWO

Barney Cheetham was trying to reach the cardboard box on the lowest shelf at the back of the large warehouse. He was thinking about last night's online video game sesh; he couldn't believe it when Nigel kept killing him. Shouts of 'I'm going to boot you in the fucking baws' were only met with peals of laughter. Sometimes Barney thought Nigel had a different side to him that nobody ever saw, a side that might pick up a hammer and bring it down on an unsuspecting skull. The chances were slim, but whenever Nigel stepped out of the control room for a pish, Barney made sure he had one eye on the door. Fuck looking at the cameras.

'Come on, for fuck's sake,' Barney said. He was

down on his knees, raking about, reaching in for the bastard at the back of the shelf. This was metal racking with wire shelves, so the boxes got all dusty. He'd already tossed half a dozen out, leaving them in the aisle so he could get in further, but no matter how hard he tried, he couldn't reach.

Bastard thing, he thought, getting right in. The hard wires dug into the palms of his hands, even through his gloves, and he was crawling now, much like he did when he was pished and trying to get into bed. The wires dug into his knees as well, prompting an idea to get knee pads for in here.

He wasn't sure what bastard had packed this shelf, but the item he wanted was the one at the back. Of course it was. Sod's law. At least it had all been inventoried, making it easier to chorie.

If the box was in this far, nobody would be in a hurry to look for the shite that was in it. The boxes hadn't been looked at since they were brought here to be stored from their original storage facility.

Now they were in here, never to be touched by human hands again, unless they were called for, which he doubted, or rifled through by he and Nigel, which he was sure of.

He got his gloved hands on the cardboard box. Large, brown, covered in dust. Some of the stuff was in smaller boxes, or file boxes, and put on a shelf that could be reached without herniating a disc. But these items had to be in a big box and were kept at the bottom.

'Barney!' a voice shouted.

Barney's instinct was to shoot his head up, and it smacked against the wires above it, just as he almost shat himself.

'You in there?' Nigel asked.

'Of course I'm fucking in here. What gave it away? The fact that I said I was going to be here or the boxes scattered about?' *'Ya daft bastard,'* he was about to add, but then thought that his friend might be standing there with a knife and the insult might just push him over the edge.

Nigel laughed. 'You got it yet?'

'Aye. I just got my hands on it. Next time, you can get in here.'

'I've got a bad back, Barney.'

'Now I've got a bad heid after I just clattered it off this fucking rack.'

Nigel laughed like he'd just watched a funny cartoon.

'I'm glad you're amused,' Barney said, shuffling slowly out.

'Christ, you've got a split in the arse of your

trousers,' Nigel said.

'Where?' Barney said, panic in his voice. He stopped shuffling back out and his right hand came round in the tight space to feel his backside.

'Bum feeler!' Nigel shouted and cracked up laughing.

'Ya bastard,' Barney said, all thoughts of Nigel being a madman now gone.

'I wish you could see your face,' Nigel said, his laughter subsiding.

Barney made it back out to the aisle, where his knees touched concrete. He stood up, his face flushed, and a look of relief swept over it as he saw that his friend had nothing more dangerous in his hand than a Twix from the vending machine.

'Is half of that for me?' he asked Nigel.

'Is it fuck. Did you give me half the money?'

There it was again, a slight shift behind the man's eyes, like his brain had slipped a gear. Then Nigel laughed. 'Of course half is for you.'

One half had the end bitten off. Barney took his gloves off and reached for the other half.

'I licked it,' Nigel said, just as Barney's finger and thumb were about to grab it. He pulled his hand back.

'I'm kidding,' Nigel said, but his smile had dropped a bit.

The manky bastard might have shoved it up his arse for all Barney knew, so he just smiled and said, 'I'm not that hungry. You have it, mate.'

'Aw, cheers, mate. That's very kind of you. Next time, I'll pay for it.' Nigel bit off another piece, leaving Barney to wonder if Nigel had dipped into the tea kitty again. The day staff would wonder where all the fucking money was going, and Barney made a mental note to bring in a box of his mother's teabags to make it look like they had actually used the money to buy tea. Nigel used to put an IOU in the jar, but that had soon gone sideways.

'Give me a hand to get these boxes back, pal. My back's giving me gyp,' Barney said, putting one hand on his back for added effect, making sure to keep it well away from the phantom rip in his trousers.

'No can do, squire. The old bawbag was just on the phone. He's on his way over. That's why I'm down here, to let him in the back door again.'

Well, I'll just do it myself, lazy wee fud. 'Mind and not bring him in here. He'd be like a kid in a sweet shop.'

'I'm no' daft, Barney.'

Since when? 'I know, pal. I'm just excited about

this big pay day. Great to have extra cash in our pockets.'

'It is that,' Nigel replied, shoving the second stick of Twix into his mouth and chewing furiously. 'I thold him to thext me when he'th here,' he said, spraying crumbs and bits of chocolate on top of the boxes that were in the aisle.

'Fuck's sake, anybody looking at these boxes in the future will wonder what shat all over them.'

'Don't make me fucking laugh,' Nigel said, swallowing and laughing at the same time. He turned and walked away, coughing and laughing some more. Barney was sure a forensics team wouldn't have to work too hard to find some DNA plastered on unsuspecting boxes.

Nigel's footsteps receded and Barney heard a door open further along. He was glad the fuckwit had remembered to turn off the security system on the door from the control room, or the next thing they knew, the finest personnel from Sighthill would be arriving in their shiny red trucks with blue flashing lights, wondering where the fire was.

Barney starting sweating, thinking about how they would explain that one away.

He slit the tape on the box with a knife and

opened the lid. Inside was the Golden Ticket, the item that some weirdo was willing to pay two grand for. This was the best they'd had since they'd started selling this stuff.

He took it out of the box, taped it back shut with the dispenser he'd brought, then carried the item along to the back door. The man was standing next to Nigel, wearing an outfit like the one Tom Baker had worn in *Doctor Who*.

'There you are, Mr Powers,' Barney said, and held out the object without letting go of it. Powers reached out to take it. 'Sorry, but same rules as the last time.'

Powers nodded, and Barney and Nigel could see the smile in amongst the rat's nest he had on his face. Then the old man put a hand in his pocket. Barney was ready to skelp him at the first sign of a weapon, or at the very least set Nigel on him, but Powers brought out nothing more dangerous than two bundles of bank notes.

He handed the money over, Barney gave him the object, and Powers turned and walked back out.

Nigel closed the door and it locked in place.

'Not a bad night's work,' Barney said.

'Not at all,' Nigel replied, taking one of the

bundles. 'Just imagine how many Twix's we could buy with this.'

You get them for fucking free, Barney was about to say, but let it go. Then he thought about what he was going to do with his half of the pay out.

TWENTY-THREE

Harry lay back on the settee, staring up at the ceiling. The film had been on for an hour or so but it felt like it had been days. It was a rom-com, Alex had told him, and he had started watching it with enthusiasm, God alone knew he had, but the romance part bored him and the comedy part was non-existent.

Alex sat on the settee with him, her hand automatically going into the popcorn bowl and feeding her mouth like she was a robot. Just the way popcorn eaters all over the world ate it.

Then a piece hit him on the nose.

He moved his head back before lifting it and looking at her. Alex laughed. 'Sorry. I was aiming for your mouth.'

He sat up. 'My mouth wasn't open.'

'Still. If it had been, that would have been a score. Sadly, it wasn't meant to be.'

He took some of the popcorn and shoved it all into his mouth, unlike his wife, who ate it one piece at a time.

'Is the film boring you?' she asked, a slight smile on her lips.

'Of course not. I'm enjoying it.'

'Liar. But thanks for trying anyway.'

'It's the least I could do since you made us popcorn.'

The front door opened and Jessica came in. She walked into the living room and smiled at them.

'You're home early,' Alex said, looking at the clock: ten past ten.

'I was tired, to be honest. It was a hard day at the nursery. Parents complaining; some not paying and falling behind. Two of the kids vomited. It was all go.'

Harry owned the nursery not far from their house in Murrayfield. He had inherited both properties from a late girlfriend, as well as her flat down near where he lived in Comely Bank.

'It's time we had a review of the staff wages,' he said.

'Oh, Harry, no, you pay more than anybody in

this game,' Jessica said. 'I'm not complaining about the job, honestly. I'm just telling you I feel tired, that's all. Bless you, though.'

'You'll be able to recharge your batteries over the Christmas holidays,' Harry said.

'I know. I'm going to make a cup of hot chocolate. You want anything?'

'I'm fine, thanks,' Alex said.

'I'm okay, thanks,' Harry said.

'Okay, then.' Jessica left the living room and went to the kitchen.

'Just as well we weren't going at it on the couch,' Alex said, giggling.

'I can't even imagine.'

'Why don't we turn off this crap film and have an early night?' Alex suggested.

'I've got a better idea. It would involve your sister.'

Alex raised her eyebrows.

'As a babysitter,' Harry clarified.

'Go on then, I'm all ears.'

Jessica was only too happy to babysit Grace. The little girl was already tucked up in bed, and if she woke up, the baby monitor would alert her.

'It's been a long time since I was here,' Alex said as they stood in the Incident room.

'Where the bloody hell are they?' Harry said, pulling out a drawer and slamming it back in.

'The keys won't have been left willy-nilly in a drawer somewhere,' Alex said.

'I bet one of those CID buggers has been arsing about with stuff in here. Christ.'

'How about in the lock box over there?' Alex nodded to a box on the top of a shelving unit sitting against a wall. There was a cork board above it where the keys were kept, defeating the whole purpose of having a lock box in the first place. Harry unlocked it and took out the set of keys he was looking for.

Then he walked over to Elvis's desk, pulled open a middle drawer and took out a buff folder. He opened it up and pulled out some photos.

'What are you looking at?' Alex asked.

'These are old crime-scene photos from a murder that happened in Orkney back in two thousand. A young girl was brutally murdered in her bedroom. Nobody was ever caught. The suspect drowned himself in the sea.'

He scattered some photos around, then stopped at one that showed the teenager covered in blood, lying on her bed. The picture had been taken from the doorway, taking in the whole room.

Harry took a photo of it with his phone before putting everything back. 'Come on, let me show you something.'

Alex looked along the corridor as they left the Incident room, switching the lights off as they went.

'Good times,' she said, nodding in the direction of their old office. The office where Harry had met Alex just a few short years ago, when he had been posted to the cold case unit.

'You know our old unit closed down, don't you?' Harry asked as they started heading for the exit.

'What? No. They closed it down? I didn't know that.'

'The University of Strathclyde work on cold cases now, allowing law students to help. There was no need for our old unit to stay open as well.'

'Jesus. But didn't you say something about you working a cold case?'

'You'll get them too. When there's not a major investigation going on, we get handed a cold case and told to work on it. Just to give us something to do.

Like the folder I just showed you. That's a case that Calvin Stewart asked us to work on.'

Outside, the night air kept getting colder. There was a sharp chill that would cut to the bone as they walked back to the car.

'Look, up there,' Alex said as she held on to Harry's arm.

He looked up like a dafty, expecting to see an alien ship. 'What? I can't see anything.'

'The sky's clear,' Alex said. 'Look at all those stars.'

'The nearest one is Proxima Centauri. It's about four light years away.'

She smiled and looked at him. 'You really know how to impress a girl. But what I was going to say is, up there is a parallel universe, where the other you and I are right now.'

'Doing what?'

'Maybe just eating popcorn and watching an old film like we were doing.'

'I wonder if they're having as much fun as we are?'

'I don't think they are. I mean, not every girl gets to see the inside of a police station on a Friday night. Unless she gets blootered, that is.'

They got into Alex's Audi A3, where there was some lingering heat.

'Where to now?' she asked.

'I told you it was a mystery.'

'Just tell me, Harry.'

'And spoil the surprise? Just follow my directions.'

TWENTY-FOUR

'I just want you to know that I don't always go back with a man to his house on the first date,' Julie said.

'I know you don't,' Dan said.

'How do you know?'

'Because you already told me over dinner. And in the bar. And in the taxi on the way up here.'

When he'd invited her home for a drink, she'd been unsure at first, knowing that this could end in disaster, but she kept the alcohol to a minimum and made sure that whenever they had a drink, Dan wasn't alone with it. It was her polis training kicking in.

She'd thought maybe he lived in a wee semi when he said his home was near the Longstone bus depot, but this was nowhere near the bus depot. It was a huge detached property off Lanark Road. There was a wooden fence with a hedge on top in front of the house.

'Keeps the riffraff from nebbing in the bedroom windows,' Dan said, nodding across the road to a neighbour's house. He laughed. 'Not really. Come on. Let's get inside.' He paid the taxi driver and the cab moved off with a clatter.

'Hear that sound?' he said, opening the gate for Julie.

'What sound?'

'The diesel taxi engine. Just wait until they're all electric. You think your utility bill's high now? Just wait until some suit somewhere shoves the price right up when we're all driving electric cars. It's about power and corruption, nothing to do with the environment. If it was, they wouldn't all be flying about in private jets.'

'You don't like the idea of a clean planet then?' Julie said as he closed the gate.

'Don't get me wrong, of course I do. I just don't like the scum politicians telling us what we can and can't do while they're making millions off us.' He took a deep breath and blew it out into the cold air. 'Listen to me, ranting on,' he said, smiling again.

'Come on, let's get you inside and we can have a nightcap.'

She laughed as he unlocked the front door. Inside, Julie was impressed with the old house. It had an immediate air of quality about it. They took their shoes off and he led her through to a huge living room. The warm air enveloped her and she immediately felt at home here. The furnishings looked quality, from the settees to the cabinets. A huge TV sat against one wall.

'You want to watch some TV?' he asked her.

'No. Let's have that nightcap and then you can tell me all about yourself.'

'I thought I'd told you all about myself over dinner?' he said with a cheeky smile, walking over to the drinks cabinet.

'That just cracked the surface. I want to know more.'

'Your wish is my command. Now, what's your poison?'

'Bacardi and Coke?'

'Sounds good.'

Dan opened the drinks cabinet and took out a bottle of Bacardi and a glass. He held up the glass for Julie to see, poured some and took a drink from it. Poured some more into another glass and handed it to her. 'I just want to assure you that you're safe,' he said, smiling at her.

'Thank you. I appreciate it.'

'Ice? I have cold cans of Coke in the fridge.'

'I'd like some ice, thanks.'

'I'll let you open the can yourself.' He left the room for a moment, then she heard some kind of movement in the hallway and thought, *That was quick*. But it wasn't Dan. It was an older man in a wheelchair.

'I thought I heard voices,' the man said, smiling at her as he manoeuvred himself into the room. He was balding but had done the modern thing and shaved what was left down to the wood.

'Oh, I'm sorry,' Julie said. 'I hope we didn't disturb you.' *Whoever you are*.

'I'm Bill. Dan's dad.'

'Oh. He didn't mention you. I'm sorry, we would have been quieter if I'd known.'

'Don't be silly. Dan didn't tell me he was bringing a young lady back home.'

'Dad! I didn't realise you were still awake,' Dan said, coming back into the room.

'I was just watching a bit of TV when I heard voices.'

'Did you think it was burglars?' Dan replied.

'Were you going to mow them down in your wheel-chair?' He laughed.

'Bloody cheek. Listen to him. But aren't you going to introduce me?'

'Of course I am. Detective Sergeant Julie Stott, this is my dad, Bill Jenkins.'

'Pleased to meet you, Bill,' Julie said.

'Likewise. But don't let me spoil your fun. I'll get back to my own room. Nice meeting you, Julie.'

'You too, Mr Jenkins.'

'Call me Bill.'

'Or the old Bill. Since you're a copper,' Dan said, and laughed at his own joke.

'His talent's wasted, isn't it?' Bill said, then left the living room.

'Hang fire and I'll get the ice and Coke,' Dan said, then left the room again. He came back a couple of minutes later with a full ice tray and an unopened can of Coke. He handed her the can, then twisted the ice cube tray and let Julie finagle a couple of cubes out.

'I'll be right back,' he said, and Julie opened the can and poured, watching the brown liquid fizzing into the Bacardi on top of the ice cubes.

She was just settling back into the settee when she heard raised voices. She got up to see what was going on but then heard Dan coming back along the hallway.

'Everything alright?' Julie said to him. 'I hope your dad isn't angry at me coming back.'

'What? Oh no, nothing like that. I gave him a telling off because he's supposed to get me to help him out of bed when he wants to get up. I worry that he'll fall, that's all.'

'Has he been in a wheelchair long, if you don't mind me asking?'

'Years now. Maybe ten or so. He likes to tell people he was a stuntman and then one of his stunts went wrong. Truth is, he was in a car accident. A drunk driver hit him and he went over a ditch. Silly bugger didn't have his seat belt on and, well, you see the result for yourself. He works from home now. He's a stockbroker.'

'He seems nice,' Julie said.

'He is. We get on well.' Dan went back to the drinks cabinet and poured himself a double malt whisky, then sat down beside her. 'Cheers.'

They clinked glasses and drank.

'How would you feel about going out with an older woman?' Julie asked. The words were blurted out like a steam train coming out of a tunnel, but as her father used to say, you can't un-ring a bell.

'How old are you, Julie?' Dan asked her.

'I just turned thirty.'

He smiled. 'I'm forty-one.'

She opened her eyes wide. 'What? No. You don't look any more than twenty-five.'

'Thank you. People are always telling me that. I look after myself. Seriously. I just turned forty-one a couple of months ago.'

'But...your dad looks so young too.'

'It runs in the family. And they had me early.'

'Does your mum live here too?' Julie asked.

Dan's smile slipped a bit. 'No. Mum died a few years ago.'

'Oh, I'm sorry, Dan.'

He smiled again. 'Don't be. She always taught me to see the brighter side of life. She would have loved you, let me tell you. And we celebrate her life, we don't dwell on her death.'

Julie lifted her glass again. 'Cheers to your mum.'

TWENTY-FIVE

'Just sit tight and I'll go and open the gate,' Harry said, and he got out of the car and ran across the road, where he unlatched a gate that was being sucked in by two high hedges. Alex was worried that some drunk was going to come flying round the bend in the road; darkness and winter driving were a lethal combination. But then she saw Harry waving wildly at her, so she put the car in gear and turned the car into the driveway fast.

She stopped and waited for her husband to close the gate and get back in the car before moving up the gravel driveway, the LED lights picking out the old house and hedges.

'The gardener's cottage is behind the hedge in front to the left,' Harry said, pointing.

'I bet this place cost a fortune,' she said.

'Close to two mil.'

'And there are plenty of people who can afford it.'

'We could afford it,' Harry said. 'If I sold the business and our two properties.'

'But could we afford a gardener to live in that cottage?'

'I've got you for that.'

'Cheeky sod,' Alex said.

'Women are equal. I was letting you know I wouldn't stop you getting the lawnmower out.'

'I would, you know. I'm younger than you are. I could do it in half the time.'

'Touché.'

She looked at him in the darkness. 'You had to pay the life insurance money back, didn't you?'

Harry nodded. 'Neil McGovern took care of it. They got their money back, with interest, and he made sure your policy didn't lapse. It's back on track again. I didn't spend any of the money, though. I just kept it in the bank.'

She smiled at him and squeezed his hand before turning off the engine and getting out.

There was a frost on the front lawn and starting to get a grip on the gravel stones. Their feet crunched as they walked towards the cottage, now in darkness as the car lights were cut off.

Alex grabbed hold of Harry's arm even though she had boots on. 'Can you imagine this being a nice castle hotel? You and me just spending the weekend, staying in bed, eating strawberries and cream –'

Harry stopped suddenly and Alex halted beside him. 'What's wrong?' she asked, all thoughts of fruit and dairy now gone.

'There's a light on in there,' he said, his voice a whisper in the cold, dark air.

'Where?' Alex said as Harry gently prised her fingers from his arm.

'The curtains have been pulled in that front room, but if you look at the top, there's a gap and you can see a light from inside.'

'Christ, here's me wittering on and there could be somebody in there.'

'I wouldn't normally say "Stay behind me", but I've been in here and know my way around.'

'Go on then. I won't argue. I feel a little bloated after dinner anyway.'

'Jesus. You could have left it at you not arguing.'

She slapped his arm. 'Let's just get a move on. I'm freezing out here.'

'Right, well, whoever's in there, they know we're

here because of the gravel, so there's no point in sneaking in. But don't go in as if we're going to have tea with the vicar. Go in with the attitude that you're going to kick the shit out of the vicar.'

'Kick vicar's head in. Check.'

'Please don't take your safety for granted.'

She smiled. 'I won't.'

He approached the door and saw it was still closed. He tried the handle. It was unlocked. *Fuck.* He opened the door and walked in, his extendable baton now out and held down at his side. He cleared the first room, then the one opposite, leaving the lights on. Next, the bathroom, which they'd surmised was the point of entry for the killer. Empty and window locked.

The light was on in the living room. Nobody was around or hiding. Whoever had been in here was long gone.

Harry had given the bedroom where the victim had been found a cursory glance a moment ago, but now as he was standing in the doorway looking in, it jumped out at him. He took his phone out and navigated to the photos and opened the one he had taken of the crime-scene photo in the office.

'So you took a photo of the photo of this crime scene?' Alex said.

'No, I took a photo of the original crime scene from Orkney, twenty-three years ago. Octavia Patterson was murdered in her bed.' He swiped to the next photo and showed her the scene from the house in Orkney, Octavia still lying naked on her bed, covered in blood.

'You see here, on the corner table, there's a lamp. It looks like an antique with a stained-glass shade. Little tassels hanging down.'

'I see that,' Alex said, looking between the photo and the room in front of her. 'I don't see it here. I mean, the room's similar, but it's not exactly the same.'

Harry swiped again. 'This is this very room after the victim and the mannequin were taken out. Look in the corner of the photo.'

She did. The lamp was there. A lamp had been sitting in the corner. 'That looks almost exactly like the one from the original crime scene.'

'Exactly. The whole room is similar to the original crime scene.' He looked at her. 'But somebody came back and took the lamp. Why?'

'Do you think somebody on the team stole it?'

'No. I think whoever killed Kenny Smith and posed him here came back for it.'

TWENTY-SIX

Getting out of bed was an Olympic sport for DI Charlie Skellett. There was some grunting, some serious rocking back and forward on the edge of the mattress, some holding the breath, then with an almighty force of will, he was up and twisting round to put two hands on the bed so he could straighten up with one final noise followed by a swift 'bastard' uttered under his breath.

Today was no exception, apart from stretching the curse out to a sharp 'Oh, ya bastard' as his knee started to ask him what the hell he thought he was playing at.

'Bugger it all to hell,' he said when he opened the curtains and looked out the bedroom window. 'It's snowing.'

'It's what?' his wife, Rose, said, her head poking out from under the duvet. Or rather, her curlers were. And her eyebrows and her eyes. Her nose was still under.

'Bloody snowing,' Skellett replied, as if he had managed to somehow say it in Spanish the first time. He turned back from the window without opening the curtains. 'I promised the kids you'd take them to the museum to see that *Dr Who* exhibition.'

'You promised them *you* would take them, before you lumbered me with going.'

'Harry McNeil is wanting us in today. You know what it's like on an active enquiry. All hands at the wheel. Even at the weekends.'

'Aye, I know how it is. I've been married to you long enough. Are you sure they would like it anyway?' Rose said.

'They're kids. What's not to like?'

'I think you would have more fun than them.'

'Away, woman. There's loads of stuff to do at the museum. I loved going there when I was a boy.'

'That was so long ago, the dinosaurs weren't extinct.'

'You're funny. Go and get the kettle on while I pee. Then I'll feed my boy.' His dog, Sir Hugo, came into the bedroom as if he'd been waiting outside the room.

'There's Daddy's boy. You needing fed or have to go for a pee?'

The dog chuffed at him.

'Right, let me get sorted first, then I'll get you out. You can give it the biscuit outside with your barking and wake up that old bawbag next door.'

'Charlie, for God's sake.'

'Well, he is. He accused me of letting Sir Hugo here take a shite on his front lawn. First of all, he's got a cheek calling that scraggy patch of weeds a lawn, and second, there are other dugs that get walked in this street. You know what? Next time he asks to borrow some black pepper or something, put itching powder in it.'

Rose tutted and lifted the duvet away and slung her legs out of the bed.

'I heard about Kenny Smith on the news,' she said, getting her dressing gown on and going through to the kitchen to flick the kettle switch.

'Aye, somebody did him up good and proper, but I can't talk about it much. Except to say there's another one. We haven't identified him yet, but we're working on it.'

'I'm not asking you to talk about it. I'm telling you what I heard on the radio.'

'Good then,' Skellett said when he was finished, coming into the kitchen. 'I'll give the boy his breakfast, then I'll shower. Put some toast on for me, love.'

'Is that all you keep me around for?' Rose asked him with a smile.

'That and...fill in the blank.'

'God, you're incorrigible.'

TWENTY-SEVEN

'What are you working on?' Angie Fisher asked Robbie Evans, looking over his shoulder. The Incident room was quiet, the rest of the team still to arrive.

Evans jumped and quickly flipped the newspaper over to page five, knocking his coffee over in the process. 'For fu–' he was about to say, thinking it was Hamish, but then the smell of perfume should have given it away.

'Oh, it's you, ma'am,' he said as she stepped back and he shot the office chair back.

'Sorry. Didn't want to disturb you, but when my second discreet cough didn't get me noticed, I thought I'd creep up on you and make you shite yourself.'

'Mission accomplished,' he said as he went over to the coffee station. He grabbed a roll of paper towels and rushed back with it, unwinding as he went.

'Here, give me some,' Angie said, and taking the wad she was offered, she started mopping up the coffee from the paper.

Evans got the rest, and one roll of towels later, everything looked shipshape, except for a very soggy newspaper.

'I always read the news online,' Angie said.

'Do you?' Evans sat back down.

'Aye. It saves it from having a cup of coffee spilled over it.'

'That's never happened to me before,' he said, glad his bacon roll had come wrapped in foil.

'I've heard that before from a man. It's more common than you think.'

'No, I meant spilling a coffee on my desk.'

'Sure you did. You weren't trying to give me some spiel like I'm some lassie who's new in the job?'

'No, of course not! I mean, I meant my coffee.'

Angie laughed. 'Relax, Robbie, I'm just pulling your short and curlies. Metaphorically speaking.'

'Oh, right.' *Thank fuck for that.*

'Unless you really did mean it?'

'Jesus, no. I have respect for all women, especially my female colleagues.'

Angie pulled up another office chair. 'Where did you recite that from? A flashcard from Tulliallan?'

'It's true. Despite what my girlfriend thought.'

'Vern?'

'You know her?' Evans asked.

'No. Calvin told me you were seeing each other. I used to work with Muckle McInsh.'

'More than seeing each other; we were engaged.'

'And I'm guessing from the way your eyes have glazed over that you're no longer planning on tying the knot?'

'Correct. Coffee, ma'am?' Evans said, standing up and walking back over to the coffee station, where he switched the kettle on.

'Ta.' She stood up and walked over to him. 'Life's hard, Robbie. Relationships are even harder. You know the secret?'

'Apparently not or else I might still be in one.'

'Two words: fuck 'em. If you're with somebody and they don't treat you with respect, fuck 'em.'

'Aye well, we split up because I was keeping her hanging on regarding the wedding. It was a sort of misunderstanding.'

'Oh?'

'Aye. She thought I wanted to get married.'

The kettle clicked off and he made two coffees.

'It's not a union made for everybody, right enough,' Angie said.

'Are you married?' Evans asked. 'If I'm allowed to ask.'

'Of course you're allowed to ask. Let me ask you: do *you* think I'm married?'

Aw, shite. Evans did a quick calculation; how quickly could he feign having to run to the men's? Like, *run* run. Like he had had too much to drink last night and now his stomach was telling him that it wasn't going to put up with his pish anymore and it had passed on all of its contents down the tube in one go?

Fuck it. Grabbing a bull by its horns might have been easier, but he decided to go for it anyway.

'You're young, in your forties I would say. Attractive in a biker bitch sort of way. You don't have a wedding ring on, but your thumb goes to your wedding finger as if there was one still there, so that's muscle memory. You want to spin it with your thumb like you used to do, but it's not there anymore. There's a slight indentation on your finger, backing my theory up. There would have to be something wrong with you to have been left on the shelf, so I would say you were married but now you're not.'

He drank some of his coffee.

'I have to admit I think I peed a little there. That was an astounding piece of detective work. Spot on. Except the biker chick part. Cheeky bastard.' She smiled as she added some milk from the carton in the fridge.

Evans grinned.

'Robbie, how come you can deduce all of that but couldn't see what was right in front of your face? That you were going to get dumped?'

'Same way somebody pokes a finger into a socket, I suppose.'

'That sounds almost logical,' Angie said as they made their way back over to the desk.

'Where did you get the roll?' she asked.

'Canteen.'

'I'll nip along in a bit and get one. You know, you surprise me, Robbie; I thought Hamish would have been in first.'

'He cycles. He's a madman, or as DCI Dunbar calls him, an organ donor.'

Just then the Incident room door banged open and the ginger man himself made an appearance, clattering a bike through. His ginger hair was wrapped in a bicycle helmet and his face was doing its fair bit to compete with the hair.

'I'm bloody knackered,' Hamish said. He looked like he'd just been dragged from a river and was waiting for a body bag. He weaved his bike round the desk, balanced it for a few seconds and then fired it towards the back of the room, where it hit the wall, wondered what it should do with itself, then thought *Fuck it, I'm knackered too* and tumbled sideways.

'You look like you enjoy riding to work,' Angie said with undisguised sarcasm.

'Trying to protect the environment,' Hamish said with a sneer. 'I nearly came off it after I hit an icy patch. And have you read about those cyclists in Edinburgh who crashed after going down the tram lines?'

Angie and Evans both shook their head.

'If we're going to cycle, then we should be like the old China, where everybody cycles. Not just me and a handful of others. I'm not going on that death-trap again. I feel like my Y-fronts are trying to give me a colonoscopy.'

Angie and Evans made a face.

'For God's sake, Hamish, it's too early in the morning for this kind of guff,' Angie said.

'Sorry, Sarge. Ma'am. I'm feeling like I need a chocolate Hobnob. I'm getting the heebie-jeebies.'

'You're giving us the heebie-jeebies, mate, just with the mental image of your underpants,' Evans said.

'I'm Type-2 diabetic. I need a wee bit of sugar.'

'There's Rich Teas in the biscuit tin,' Evans suggested.

'Rich Teas? Nothing with chocolate?'

'Aye, there's chocolate biscuits, but unfortunately for you, they're in the canteen,' Angie said. 'You can get me a bacon roll while you're there. Wash your hands first.' She fished out a couple of pound coins and handed them over. 'Ketchup.'

'Not brown sauce?' Hamish asked.

'Do I look like I come from Edinburgh? Bloody heathen, talking filth like that.'

Hamish blew out a breath and took his bike helmet off, then punted it over to land beside the bike; clearly, neither would come into contact with his extremities again.

'Just relax, Hamish, and get a cup of coffee. The others will be in soon, I'm sure.'

TWENTY-EIGHT

The drive through from Edinburgh to Glasgow didn't take long in the early-morning Saturday traffic.

'I'd appreciate it if you didn't say anything about Lynn staying at my place,' Calvin Stewart said to Harry. 'Well, *your* place but where I'm renting.'

'I won't. And it's your place. None of my business who you have staying, unless it's a gang of bikers who're going to tear the place up or Devil-worship.'

'No fear of that, Harry, son. Lynn appreciates it, though she hates that somebody might think she's running away.'

'Nobody knows where she is, and those who do don't think anything of the sort. I mean, look at Alex; she was in protective custody for nearly a year.'

'We do what we've got to do. Thank Christ

Davie is going to be okay. He could easily have started with stabbing Lynn.'

They made quick time to the hospital and were surprised to see Davie Ross sitting up in bed, smiling. Then Joan Devine came out of the bathroom.

'If I didn't know better, I would think you were creating your own version of the mile high club,' Stewart said. 'But there's got to be two of you for it to count.'

'Hey, ya mucky bastard,' Ross said.

Joan chuckled. 'With his bad back and me not being as flexible as I used to be, I think we'd be in the *Guinness Book of Records.*'

'Don't encourage him, for God's sake,' Ross said.

'You boys wanting a seat?' Joan asked.

'I'm fine, thanks,' Harry said.

'Harry,' Stewart said, 'this is Deputy Fiscal Joan Devine and Chief Super Davie Ross, who I was telling you about.'

'Nice to meet you, ma'am,' Harry said, shaking Joan's hand.

'It's Joan. I'll be retired soon.'

'Aye, Davie and Joan are going to be shacking up in Spain soon, like a couple of cocaine smugglers. On the run and desperate.'

'Christ, shut your hole, Calvin,' Ross said. Then he looked at Harry. 'Pleased to meet you, son.'

'Likewise, sir.' They shook hands.

'Calvin called and told me you're working a case that might be related to one I worked on in Orkney years ago,' Ross said.

'That's right, sir. Our victim was screwed to metal plates that put him in a pose like he was a killer. He was holding a knife and *his* victim was a female mannequin. Covered in paint to simulate blood.'

'The victim who was in the house in Orkney was a young girl. Eighteen, she was. Lynn and I flew up there. But we got nowhere. It was like they closed ranks and couldn't wait for us to piss off so they could deal with it in-house, like they were in their own wee world. The obvious suspect had apparently committed suicide by walking into the sea, but no body was ever found.'

'Do you think he actually did walk into the sea?' Harry asked.

'He was never heard from again. Maybe they got hold of the bastard; who knows? Maybe they found him that night and dealt with him. Made it look like a suicide.' Ross stared into space, either thinking back to that time or maybe contemplating the mile high club thing after all; Harry couldn't be sure.

'I was at the crime scene in Edinburgh,' Harry said, 'and I thought it looked familiar. You had asked Calvin to look into the Orkney cold case and young Elvis – DC Colin Presley – had the files and we were all looking at the case. I went back to our crime scene last night with my wife, who's also a detective, and I saw that the current crime scene is an exact replica of the Orkney one. Except for one little detail.'

The other three looked at him.

'Come on, Harry, don't keep us in suspense here,' Stewart said, keeping the swearing to a minimum for Joan's sake.

'At both crime scenes there was an antique lamp by the bed. But last night, I found it was gone. Somebody went back and took it.'

'Why the hell would somebody do that?' Ross asked.

'I don't know. I'm going to have my team question everybody who was there.'

'That's fucking shan if one of those bastards choried it,' Stewart said, letting his tongue slip.

'It is.'

'That new bastard, Callum Craig. You trust him?' Stewart asked Harry.

'Who *can* I trust nowadays?'

'Me, ya cheeky bastard.'

Harry smiled. 'That goes without saying. I'd even stretch so far as to say I trust DCS Ross and Joan, because you vouch for them, but when other professionals come into your life, well, you just don't know, do you?'

'The lad's got a point,' Ross said. 'Meantime, while you're waiting to grill that Craig bastard, I'd like you lot to get your arse up to Orkney. I haven't retired yet, and before they put an interim DCS in place, I'm authorising this look into the cold case. That's what they want us to do nowadays, instead of sitting about with our thumbs up our arses. So Calvin, put a team together and get them up there. Have a poke around.'

'It's probably going to be at least a one-night stay,' Stewart said.

'I'm sure there are some hotel rooms you can book. Or a B&B. Just make it happen, even if you have to bunk in with some of the uniforms.'

'I'll have Alex drive me through some changes of clothes,' Harry said.

'I have some here already. At…another place.

Here.' Stewart didn't make eye contact with anybody.

'At Lynn's place, you mean?' Joan said.

'Well, if you're going to be nitpicky about it, Joan, then...well...'

'For God's sake, Calvin Stewart. We all know she's your girlfriend. Stop acting like a wee school laddie.'

'Aye, well, at Lynn's place. There. Are you happy?'

'I am,' Joan said. 'You go and get your skids, the clean ones mind, not the ones that are festering in the washing machine, and pack a couple of shirts.'

'Festering?' Stewart said. 'Everything is clean, I'll have you know. Ready to be picked up.'

'Wear some fucking long johns,' Ross said. 'That wind will rip your goolies right off.'

'Language, Davie, there's a lady here,' Stewart said.

'You swore first,' Ross quickly replied.

'She's no' my girlfriend, though, is she? A wee bit of decorum there, pal. Or else she might just decide to see if the grass really is greener on the other side. Eh, Joan?'

Joan rolled her eyes. 'I don't think Davie's got

anything to fear, have you, love?' She smiled at the DCS.

'Suit yourself. Don't come crying to me when you're all sunburnt in Spain and old lazy-baws there is still hungover at two in the afternoon.'

'Less of the old. Just remember I'm still a rank above you,' Ross said.

'Aye, aye.' Stewart looked at Harry. 'We'd better get the ball rolling, Harry, son. The sooner we get a flight up there, the better.'

'I'll call control and let them know to get onto Business Support so they can book your flight. There's probably one going this afternoon,' Ross said.

'Good job.'

'Tell them the fiscal's office is pushing for it,' Ross said. 'If they give you any guff, I'll call the chief himself. He knows Joan very well.'

'Right then. We'll get to the station and give them a heads-up, then you can call me with the details after you've called Business Support,' Stewart said.

'Will do.'

'Nice meeting you both,' Harry said as they said their goodbyes.

Stewart made a telephone out of his thumb and

pinkie and mouthed 'Call me' to Joan as Ross stuck up two fingers. Stewart laughed as they left the room.

'I like DCS Ross a lot,' Harry said. 'We're short of a DCS just now. I hope we get one like him. Man or woman I don't care as long as they get the job done.'

'Me too.' Stewart thought of Lynn McKenzie. A woman who always got the job done. She and Angie Fisher would make a good team. With DI Lisa McDonald.

'Don't spare the horses, Harry. Now I'm getting hungry.'

TWENTY-NINE

The door to the Incident room opened again.

'What are you pair of tits doing here?' Calvin Stewart said. Then he saw Angie. 'Not you, obviously. I meant those two reprobates.'

'Robbie and Hamish got here early,' Angie explained. 'Hamish is going to the canteen for a roll for me.'

'Get me one too, son.'

'Ketchup or brown?' Hamish said.

'Brown? Are ye daft? You think I'm from Morningside or something? And get one for DCI McNeil. He'll be here in a minute. He's just making a call. Ketchup on both.'

'Ketchup it is. Robbie?'

Evans shook his head. 'I've had one, thanks.'

'Put your hand in your pocket and pay the man,' Angie told Stewart.

Stewart tutted and handed over a tenner. 'Don't come back here and tell me you had a fucking blackout and can't remember if you got my change or not.'

Hamish nodded and left the Incident room.

'What's up with him? He looks like he's been sweating buckets. Has he been looking at lassies on TikTok again?'

'He cycled into work,' Angie explained, taking a seat at a computer. Evans sat down at his.

'Cycled? Fuck me. I can barely make it into my car in the morning. I mean, power to him, saving a whale or whatever, but coming to work wringing, feeling like you've pished yourself, isn't for me. I'll drive, every time.'

'Were you staying here overnight?' Evans asked. 'Or did you go back to Edinburgh?'

'Not that you're a nosey bastard or anything, but if you must know, I stayed at my place in Edinburgh last night. Where else would I have stayed?'

'You're welcome to stay with me and my maw if you like.'

'Talk shite. I thought you were shacking up with young Vern?'

The door opened and Stewart thought it was Ginger with the rolls, but it was Jimmy Dunbar. 'Robbie and Vern split up,' Dunbar said.

'Split up?' Stewart said. 'She was the best thing that happened to you, son. Whatever cock-and-bull story you come up with for why she booted your baws out of her bed, you'd better rethink things and beg her to take you back. Or else you'll end up marrying your auntie.'

'For God's sake, Calvin,' Angie said.

'It's true. You met Vern? If I wasn't in a relationship, I'd take her out.'

'Who are you in a relationship with?' Evans asked.

'None of your bloody beeswax who I'm in a relationship with. Bloody nebbing.'

'Is it a subscription-based relationship?' Evans asked.

'Shut your hole. That'll be something you'll be getting used to. At least you won't have to go to the gym to work on your biceps.'

Angie and Dunbar laughed.

'Anyway, ya mucky wee bastard, we've got work

to do. Harry and I popped in to see Davie Ross,' Stewart said.

'How's he doing?' Dunbar asked.

'Who? Harry or Davie Ross?'

'Davie.'

'I'm just pulling your pisser, Jimmy. He's making good progress.'

'Who? Harry or Davie Ross?' Evans said, trying not to grin.

Stewart looked at him. 'I'm glad you're amused, Evans. DCS Ross wants a team to go to Orkney. Today. We're flying up. Business Support were on the ball and they got tickets booked on a flight out of Glasgow Airport this afternoon. There was a delay because of technical problems with the plane, so it's not leaving until this afternoon, otherwise we wouldn't be going until tomorrow morning. There's five of us going. You're one of them.'

Evans stood up. 'Come on, sir, I'm begging you. Please. Take Lisa McDonald. She doesn't mind flying. I hate it. I'll die on the plane. Die of fear.'

'Lisa's running this department while we're gone. Her and Gingie-baws are going to be holding the fort. I've already called Lisa in and explained what she'll be doing, and it's not sitting her arse in a plane seat.'

'Oh, God,' Evans said. 'If I've ever said anything to offend you, *ever*, sir, I would like to sincerely apologise, and I will never say another derogatory word again.'

'Do you promise?' Stewart said.

'Yes, yes I do.'

'Good to hear. Now, get home and pack a bag; you're still going.'

'Aw, fu...' Evans looked at Angie. 'Fiddle.'

'And when your old maw sees you packing, tell her it's because you're going back to Vern. After your wee trip to Orkney.'

'Vern's never going to take me back, unless we get married,' Evans replied.

'What are you planning on doing for the rest of your life?' Stewart said. 'Joining a monastery?'

'I like being a free bird,' Evans said.

'Tell yourself that twenty years from now when you're in your fifties, your hair's gone, you wear a sleeveless sweater to the train-spotting club and the only woman you're getting comes with a puncture-repair kit. But that's your choice, son. Be a sad bastard if you want.'

Evans stood looking in the direction of the white-board, but it seemed his eyes were seeing something else. Maybe his life going down the toilet, or his friends calling him a 'confirmed bachelor'. 'If you'll excuse me for a minute, I have a phone call to make.'

'It better no' be to your fucking auntie Anne.'

'Way ahead of you, boss.'

'Good lad. Now, where's Ginger-heid with the fucking rolls?'

THIRTY

DI Frank Miller looked out of his living room window down to the High Street and there it was: not only the coldest December in twelve years but the icing on the cake had come waltzing in – snow.

Harry McNeil had called and said he was going through to Glasgow to talk to a DCS there about a cold case Elvis had been working on that Calvin Stewart had asked him to look into. Miller himself had been working on a cold case involving a murdered prostitute from the eighties. The team had been split into two and each of them had worked on a separate case.

Harry had also told him about a lamp that had been taken from a crime scene. Christ, it was bad enough that a doughnut politician had got himself murdered without somebody fucking about with the crime scene.

'You'll be going into the office today, I assume?' said Kim, his wife, as she came into the living room.

He turned to face her. 'Yeah. We're all going in. Harry's away through in Glasgow, and he called to say they're going to Orkney. Revisiting an old crime scene back from the Millennium.'

'You know that was a farce, right? Celebrating the year two thousand. The proper celebration should have been at the end of that year.'

'Agree to disagree, sweetheart.'

'I love a good conspiracy theory.'

'Me too, but it's my job as your husband to debunk some of the nonsense that comes out of you.'

She playfully slapped his arm. 'I'm always right.'

'I'm glad you think so. Your mum and dad will be waiting. And so will the girls. I don't know who's going to be more excited about the *Dr Who* exhibition, you or them.'

'My dad's looking forward to it too. He was a big fan.'

'I'm sure you'll all have fun. Tell your parents I said hi.'

'It's a pity you're working. You would have enjoyed it.'

'You can enjoy it for both of us.'

It was organised chaos as the girls ran about, finishing breakfast and waiting for Grandma and Grandpa to arrive.

'I'll leave you to it then,' Miller said.

'Thanks, honey. You enjoy yourself at work.'

He laughed. 'I will.'

He went downstairs to his car and his phone rang. It was Callum Craig, head of forensics.

'Morning, Frank. I just got the prints back from the lab. They were a bit backed up yesterday, so they worked on them this morning.'

'You get a hit?'

'We did. His name's Billy Ferguson. Lives in Edinburgh. I'll text you the exact address. He's on file because of an assault charge years ago.'

'Thanks, Callum.'

THIRTY-ONE

Alex drove Harry to Glasgow Airport, while the others went in Stewart's car.

'Frank Miller called me earlier when we were in the Incident room,' Harry said. 'The second victim's name is Billy Ferguson.'

'What do you know about him?'

'Not a lot just yet. He was arrested for assault a few years ago so his prints were in the system. Coincidence: he comes from Orkney.'

'And now somebody's murdered him and Kenneth Smith in the same way.'

'I'm assuming they were friends or acquaintances.'

'Ask around when you get to Orkney.'

'I intend to.'

They got out of the car and met round the back.

'I wish you were coming with us,' he said. 'Maybe next time.'

She nodded. 'I think I packed clean underwear,' she said as Harry grabbed the bag from the back.

'If you haven't, I'll just go commando and hope nobody's looking when I'm doing my exercises at the hotel window in the scud.'

'You'll have the whole island on shutdown if you do that.'

'I'll just keep myself occupied in other ways then.'

'A good book?'

'Correct. It's on the Kindle app on my phone.' He closed the boot of the car and laid his small suitcase on the ground. 'I'm going to miss you.'

'Me too.'

'Hopefully just a couple of nights, then we'll be back home.'

'You've got a whole team back here waiting to help. Myself included, even though I work in Fife.'

'This is a puzzle we're trying to work out, a puzzle that was started twenty-three years ago.' The air was cold and he shrugged his shoulders, trying to keep the heat in.

'Take care, Harry. I love you.'

'I love you too.' He picked up his bag, kissed her and walked into the terminal.

The others were waiting for him. Robbie Evans was chewing on a fingernail, his face pale.

'Hey, folks, how are we doing?'

'Shite, but thanks for asking, sir,' Evans said. 'I think I'm going to pass out. Just giving you a heads-up.'

'Stop talking shite, Evans,' Calvin Stewart said. 'There's a wee lassie over there staring at you. She's got a wee wheeled case and she looks excited to be getting on a plane. She's wondering why you're being such a dick.'

'Tell her she can go to Orkney. Bring her parents, make a real holiday out of it.'

'She'd be more useful than you.'

'I get airsick. I've been saying this for hours.'

'Talk pish. Tell him, Jimmy.'

Dunbar said, 'He does get sick, sir. Remember the time we flew to the islands on the small plane? The guy was hosing it out for a week.'

'This is a much bigger plane,' Stewart said. 'You'll be fine. It's a bus with wings.'

'A bus with wings?' Angie said. 'I wish.'

'Wait, what?' Evans started to say, but they were moving along now.

The bus with wings had propellers. Inside, the seats were configured with one seat across from two. Dunbar was sitting at the window with Harry on the aisle, Stewart and Evans behind. Angie sat across from Stewart.

'If you don't mind me saying, Evans, you're a bit of a fat bastard now.'

'This is hardly a jumbo jet.'

'You're the only fucking thing that's jumbo on here. Move over a bit. I bet you're one of those bastards who takes the armrest at the pictures.' Stewart tutted and wished he hadn't suggested sitting next to Evans to, as he eloquently put it, 'slap the shite out of him if he starts his pish'. 'You'd better no' fucking puke on me, boy.'

'I'll give you plenty of advance warning.'

'You'll give me fuck all. Just look out the widow and you'll see there's nothing to be scared of. Nancy boy.'

'Aw, fuck off,' Evans said under his breath.

'What?'

'I said, we're about to take off.'

'Wee bastard.'

The plane was pushed back and it taxied to the runway, where it sat for a few seconds.

'Jimmy, if we go down in the sea, I want you to know that it was a pleasure working with you. Just before we hit the water and explode in a fireball, like, text Cathy and tell her she's magic,' Evans said.

'We're not going down in a fireball, for God's sake.'

'Aye, Jimmy,' Stewart said, 'text Cathy and tell her you owe me five hundred quid and if I live, she can square up with me. No rush. At the wake will do.'

'We're all doom and bloody gloom,' Harry said.

'Aye, you're starting to give me the bloody jitters now,' Angie said. 'Relax, Robbie.'

'Yes, ma'am.'

'How come you listen to her and not me?' Stewart complained.

'She's nicer than you. No offence.'

'Offence taken. What was all that pish in the office where you said you were never going to make another derogatory remark to me?'

'That's when I thought you were going to let me stay. Now, all bets are off.'

'Aye, we'll see about that, ya wee bastard.'

The plane started moving. Evans pointed to one

of the engines as the propellers spun so fast it seemed that they would surely fly off.

'Look at that engine. It's got black stuff on the side. It's going to go on fire.'

'It's just oil, muppet. Did you think they were going to paint it just for you?'

Evans snapped his head round. 'You said this plane was delayed. I bet there was an oil leak. How could they fix it so fast?' His eyes went wide. 'I want off. Tell them to stop.'

'Aye, I'll tell the captain just to go back now, will I?'

'Aye, do it. Tell him to slow down –' Evans's mouth dropped open as he was thrown back into his seat as the plane left solid ground. Then his eyes rolled back in his head and it slumped forward.

'That'll quieten him down for an hour or so,' Stewart said to Angie. She smiled and looked over at the DS.

'Poor lad,' she said.

The flight was over an hour and Evans was still snoring when they descended. The plane bumped on touchdown. He awoke with a start and was about to shout when Stewart put a hand on his chest. 'We've landed. And not in the sea.'

'Oh. Nice. I told you we'd be okay.' Evans looked at Stewart.

'We *are* fine. You're the one with drool hanging out of his mouth. And I think you might have pished yourself.'

'What?' Evans looked down at the front of his trousers. 'For God's sake, Calvin.'

'It's Superintendent Stewart to you, ya wee bawbag.'

The plane taxied to the terminal and a small flat-bed truck reversed up to the cargo door and two men started emptying the bags onto it. The detectives disembarked and walked into the small terminal, which could have been a Customs drugs warehouse with a wee bit of imagination, but the 'Welcome to Kirkwall Airport' was reassuring.

'Welcome to the coldest place on earth,' Harry said, digging his hands into his pockets as the cold wind sprang at them.

'There goes our Harry, starting off the trip on a negative note,' Stewart said. 'You'll be happy to know that we have expenses for here, son. We might find a wee place to get blootered. Maybe the hotel's got a bar.'

'I heard they banned alcohol here starting last January first,' Angie said.

'What?' Stewart said. 'Jimmy, get your phone out and check that. Evans seems to have pissed off somewhere. Probably to wash the skid marks out of his Ys.'

'I'm just kidding, ya daft sod,' Angie said.

'You know what? Bloody Motherwell's getting a phone call when we get back. You mark my words. Insubordination, talking pish, you name it, your DCS is going to be getting a roasting.'

'From a DSup?'

'No. Davie Ross will be my voice, don't you worry.'

The limo service that was waiting for them was a Police Scotland uniform. No sign held up with their names, no eager waving. Just a bearded man in a uniform.

'I think they're taking the piss,' Stewart said after they had collected their luggage.

'How do you mean?' Angie said.

'Sending this reprobate out to pick us up. He looks like he's fucking daft. Probably lives in his mother's spare room, playing online games or knitting sweaters for dugs.' Stewart looked at Dunbar. 'Here, you've got a dug, Jimmy. You're in luck. Maybe if you put in an order now, Norman Bates will run you up a sweater for your dug before we leave.'

229

'He looks older than me,' Harry said.

'And me,' Angie said.

'What's your point?' Stewart said. 'There's probably a lack of women round here. I bet a lot of men have to stay with their folks, scrounging off their pension money.'

'Christ, it's not Victorian times, sir,' Dunbar said.

'Mark my words. They see the big city boys coming to upset their playpen, and it rubs them the wrong way. Upsets their daily bingo sesh in the station. There's too many of us to play in their dominoes league. And yes, I'm just talking about the polis here.'

Stewart stopped his spinner case for a moment. 'Where's that daft bastard Evans got to?'

They saw him coming out of the men's toilets further back, wiping his mouth with the back of his hand.

'Clarty bastard's probably just tossed his bag. I'm not sitting downwind of him in the motor,' Stewart said. 'Fight amongst yourselves, but I'm sitting up front with Dafty.'

They started walking again and Stewart walked up to the uniform. 'Detective Superintendent Stewart.'

'No, Sergeant Williams,' the uniform replied.

Stewart looked at Dunbar and shook his head in a 'See? I told you the bastard was daft' way.

Stewart decided to give the man another chance before booting him in the bollocks.

'I'm Stewart, son, and I hope for your sake you're not taking the fucking piss.'

The smile dropped from somewhere in the bushy beard and went into hiding.

'You're the Glasgow lot. Sorry. I was looking for...somebody different.'

'Did you think she's Snow White and we're four dwarfs?' Stewart said, nodding to Angie. 'Maybe we should have worn funny hats.'

The man's big belly jiggled as he gave out a nervous laugh. 'No, no, we seem to have got off on the wrong foot, sir. Please, come this way.'

Evans caught up with them.

'You okay?' Angie asked him.

'I was just having a wee drink. My mouth was like sandpaper.'

'Did you puke?'

'No, thank God. That's all I need. DSup Stewart would never let me live it down.'

'That's true. If you ever do, deny everything.'

Outside in the car park, the wind was coming in off the water.

'This is DCIs Dunbar, McNeil and Fisher. Three for the price of one. DS Robbie Evans at the back.'

'Oh, I'm very pleased to meet you all, sir,' Williams said. 'Welcome to our island. Did you know the archipelago –'

'No, I didn't. Do you moonlight as a tour guide?'

'No, sir.'

'Well, save that spiel for when you're standing in front of the mirror. Now, where's our transport, and don't tell me it's a horse and cart.'

'And we wonder why the locals think we're a bunch of wankers,' Dunbar said to Evans.

'Don't accept a cup of coffee from any of them.'

'What are you two whispering about? Deciding where you're going out on the lash tonight? Not without the rest of us, you don't.'

'I was just wondering if the booze is dear up here, sir,' Evans said.

'You toss your bag in the bogs and now you're talking about getting pished? I have to admit, Evans, I didn't think you were that brave, but we've all been there.'

Angie cleared her throat. 'Excuse me?'

'Aye, you too. I've seen you pished. All sea legs and sea shanties.'

'Once or twice.'

Stewart laughed. 'Keep telling yourself that.'

'It's the police minibus here, sir,' Williams said.

'I gathered that, what with the blue and yellow bits stuck on it. And that other gibberish. Mind you, it does say "Polis", so somebody did their homework.'

Williams unlocked it and they got the doors opened and slung the luggage in the back.

'I'm sitting up front,' Stewart told Williams. 'I've been told I have to write a report on your driving skills.'

'Well, sir, let me assure you that my driving is very much up to Police Scotland standards.'

'What about the Welsh polis? They think your driving skills are up to snuff?'

'Err, well, I'm not really sure, to be honest.'

'Relax, pal, I'm just kidding. If you don't put us through a hedge, that'll do.'

'I won't even go above the limit.'

They climbed in and the heaters were put on, but the heat had obviously gone on strike and was waiting for better working conditions. They left the airport, heading north, then Williams turned into a one-lane road, fields on either side. Stewart could see hills in the distance from his vantage point of the front passenger seat. There were passing spaces, there in case of the off chance that there actually *was* life on the island. Houses appeared on the horizon, then they were at another main road. They turned right and there was a view of Kirkwall in the distance.

'How long you been working up here, son?' Harry asked from the back.

'Twenty-five years now, sir. My wife comes from round these parts.'

'You'll remember the lassie who was murdered then?' Stewart said.

'I do that, sir. I had just passed my probation. Terrible thing it was.'

'I'll be wanting to talk to you in greater detail, back at the station,' Stewart said. 'I'm assuming vehicles have been put at our disposal?'

'Indeed. Two unmarked patrol cars are waiting for you. I'll drive you over there after you've checked in.'

Williams slowed as they came into the town and the speed limit dropped. Two streets past the distillery he turned right and drove them up to the hotel.

'Lynnfield Hotel and Restaurant,' Stewart said. 'Business support did us proud, boys and girl.' He turned in his seat. 'They got us five rooms, so nobody will have to share a room. Thank fuck.'

They got out and took their luggage into the hotel, with Williams promising Stewart he would wait.

'I would usually threaten an insubordinate officer with a transfer up here, but how do you threaten somebody who already lives here?' Stewart said to Angie as they wheeled their luggage into the reception.

'Threaten to transfer him to Glasgow. He wouldn't last five minutes there.'

'Or worse, Motherwell.' He grinned at her.

'You're funny, Calvin Stewart, you know that?'

'I do actually. I'm glad I can still make a woman smile.'

'Only if she's at gunpoint.'

They booked in and were climbing the stairs when Stewart looked back at Evans. 'Thank God we don't have to share a room with Pavement Pizza McGhee there.'

'I'm fine now that I'm on steady ground,' Evans said.

They got up to the first landing and Stewart unlocked his door and walked in.

'Is this a suite?' Evans said, pushing past and walking in.

'It is that, son. Now get oot.'

Evans dropped his case, then put a hand over his mouth and felt the world tilt on its axis. 'Oh shite,' he said between his fingers, then ran across to the en-suite bathroom, dropped to his knees and lifted the toilet seat. Then he heaved.

'Evans, ya smelly bastard! Fuck me, you're giving us all the boak out here. That's fucking stinking. Christ, they'll have to evacuate the place now. God Almighty. Get this place cleaned up, ya manky hoor.'

The others had been craning their necks in through the doorway to see what was happening, but the smell became too much.

'He said he's alright now,' Stewart said, tutting, 'then he goes and throws his ring.'

Harry, Dunbar and Angie moved then, afraid that Stewart might suggest a room swap.

'Thank Christ there's a few hours until dinner or else I'd be eating fuck all.'

THIRTY-TWO

Julie Stott felt like shite when she woke up. Her head hurt and her mouth tasted like she'd been sucking an ashtray and she didn't even smoke.

She felt her heart hammer in her chest as she wondered if Dan had given her a roofie, but no, it wasn't as if she couldn't remember anything from the night before.

In fact, Dan had been the perfect gentleman. It was *her* who had felt like taking him upstairs, but he said that wasn't what he was after. He didn't treat women like that. She remembered him saying that and thought it was refreshing to meet a man like that.

It was also frustrating. She hadn't had a boyfriend in a long time. Maybe the next time they went out to dinner, she would invite him back here, to her place. She'd make sure it was clean, and no knickers were lying about as she waited for them to magically walk to the laundry basket.

She rolled over and looked at the bedside clock; after one thirty. In the afternoon! Christ, where had the day gone? Wasn't she supposed to be in at work? Yes, she thought she was supposed to be there, working on the Kenneth Smith murder.

Dan had been asking her all about becoming a police officer, then the conversation had turned to the Smith murder. He was a good listener, and in her opinion he would make a good copper. She hoped he was going to apply soon, so she could help him with the entrance exam.

She got up out of bed, gingerly, sitting on the edge of the mattress at first, then risking standing up, glad to see it was her own carpet underneath her feet and that she hadn't spent the night in a strange bedroom.

She went to the bathroom and showered, then got dressed before going through to the kitchen to fix...what? Brunch? Nope. Too late for that. No matter what it was called, she made do with toast.

She got her phone from the charging pad, wondering if Dan had sent her a text. She felt a flutter at the thought, but when she picked it up and looked at the screen, there was nothing. No text, no missed phone call, nothing.

Should she call him?

God no. That would smack of desperation.

She would go up to the house. Apologise to him for getting blootered. He wouldn't mind her dropping in on him. He would be pleased to see her. He just didn't want to look desperate by sending her a text or leaving a voice message. She got that. She would go and see him and tell him not to feel embarrassed.

But first, she had to call Charlie Skellett because she was meant to be at work.

'Hi, Charlie?'

'If you're calling about double glazing, I have it. And I have a warranty for my car.'

'You're funny. You know it's me, don't you?'

'Of course I do. Your name came up.'

'I won't be in today. I'm sorry, but I'm feeling sick.'

'Okay, I'll mark it down that you called in sick. Take an aspirin and go back to bed. That's the best advice I can give you, Julie.'

'I will, Charlie. Thanks for that.'

'Nae bother. Get well soon.'

She hung up. Good old Charlie. He could have

chewed her out since he was the DI in charge while Harry McNeil was away, but he didn't. Bless him.

She grabbed her car keys, but then thought better of it and called for an Uber to take her up to Colinton.

She sat back in the car, asking the driver if he minded if she opened the window a bit, even though it was December, and he was fine with that.

'I don't know the exact street,' she explained. 'I looked at Google Maps and I think it's round the corner a bit. I had a wee bit too much to drink last night.'

'No problem, miss. We'll find it.'

Round in circles for a little bit until she was sure they had the right house. She remembered the tall bushes on top of the wooden fence.

'This is it,' she said. 'Thank you for your patience.'

'No problem.'

She paid him and got out, and she stood and looked at the gate as the car moved away. It had been snowing, but it hadn't stuck to the roads and the pavements just had a dusting. The sky was dull and was the colour of dirty bathwater.

Should she just walk up to the front door and knock and shout 'Surprise!' when Dan answered, or call him? *Maybe call him so he doesn't get the feeling you're a stalker,* she told herself, taking her mobile out of her bag.

She dialled his number – now in her contacts list – and listened to it ring. And ring. And ring. No voicemail. Just ringing.

Keeping her phone in her hand, she opened the gate and walked up the path, careful not to slip on the wet flagstones. She noticed other footprints in the snow. Obviously, he had been out. Was he back home now, or maybe dodging about Princes Street like a lot of other people who only had the weekends off?

She walked up to the front door and saw that it wasn't closed all the way. Maybe he was in after all.

She gently nudged it and it swung open easily.

'Hello?' she shouted. 'Dan? Are you here?' She stepped into the hallway and listened. There was no sound coming from inside. Maybe Dan and his father had gone out and hadn't shut the door properly? No, there weren't any wheelchair tracks in the snow outside. Even with footprints messing them up, there would have been a trace of tyre tracks, surely?

She walked right in, pushing the door closed behind her, and went into the living room where they'd been last night. It was empty.

'Hello?' she said again. No reply.

Then she heard something coming from the hall-way. A slight sound, like something being muffled on the carpet.

She turned at the sudden cold draft coming along the hallway and her breath caught in her chest.

He was standing there. The same man Dan had described.

He wore a hat and a long, dark coat with a multi-coloured scarf round his neck. The beard looked scruffy and unkempt, and the round glasses looked too small for his face.

Tom Powers.

He was tall, she could see that, and she also saw the long-bladed knife he was holding in his right hand, with blood on it. She looked down at his feet and saw his boots. Could she outrun him? Fight or flight. She turned and ran.

Then she found out that he was fast.

He caught her before she even reached the kitchen, and a hand turned her round.

She didn't see the fist before it connected with her jaw.

THIRTY-THREE

It was dark by the time they left the hotel.

'It gets dark at about three thirty or so in the winter,' Williams said.

'It's not technically winter for another ten days,' Stewart said.

'I'll tell the island that and see if the sun can stay out a wee bit longer while you're here, shall I, sir?'

Stewart's head was filled with so many replies, it hurt his brain, but he kept them from leaving the trap. They still needed this fat bastard to show them the ropes round here.

The Kirkwall police station was a decent size and looked like a small block of flats. It shared the car park with the fire and ambulance station.

'There's the bus station across the road,' Evans said. 'Maybe I could go back on the bus.'

'The ferry will have you bobbing and weaving worse than the plane.'

'You get airsick then, young Robbie?' Williams asked from the driver's seat of the minibus, as if he'd known the young detective for years.

'Aye, I do that, William.'

Harry looked at Jimmy Dunbar. Sergeant William Williams.

'Here's a wee tip before you fly home: a wee nip. Not a sesh, just a wee nip. Puts a lining on the stomach. My old boy swore by it.'

'And some fucking mouthwash wouldn't go amiss either,' Stewart said. 'You're honking the minibus out.'

'I popped a Tic Tac,' Evans complained from the back seat, where he had been banished. 'And I brushed my teeth. I have to say, sir, your towels are nice and soft.'

'I'm going to burn the bastards when I get back now you've had your filthy mitts all over them. And other parts of your body, no doubt.' Stewart looked across at Williams, who was giving him a funny look. 'Eyes on the road, son.'

Williams guided the van into the polis station car park. 'Here we are, lads and lass. Tips for the driver very much appreciated,' he said with a laugh.

'Here's a tip: don't let Robbie Evans anywhere near your fucking room.'

They piled out and were taken through to the back and into the Incident room, which was a decent size, Harry noted.

Three people were sitting at desks with computers.

'Heads up, these are our visitors from the mainland,' Williams said. 'DC Toby Harrison.'

Harrison lifted a finger and nodded. 'How do.'

'DC Susan Robertson.'

'Hello,' Susan said with a smile.

'Last, and very much least, DS Sean Fletcher.'

Fletcher stood up. 'Good to have you all here. I'm the highest-ranking detective on the island, so just let me know what you need. We were given a heads-up that your visit here involves the Octavia Patterson murder, so we've got whatever files we have on that. The main stuff will be with the MIT in Inverness, who dealt with it.'

'That's fine, son, thanks.' Stewart turned to Dunbar. 'Jimmy, introduce us all.'

Dunbar rattled off their names and ranks.

'We'll be here overnight, obviously, and we'll go through some of the files tomorrow, but today I'd like us to break up into teams and visit some of the people involved,' Stewart said. 'Harry, you're with me. I want to go and look at the crime scene, if the people there will let us into their house.'

'They will. I already made the call,' Fletcher said. 'It's Octavia's parents. They still live in the house.'

'Good man,' Stewart said. 'Now, the suspect for the murder was Angus Smart, the victim's teacher and boyfriend. Who disappeared after the murder.' He looked at Angie. 'Maybe you and Jimmy could go and talk to Smart's brother. Take Evans. I read that he was interviewed, but nothing stuck with him. And he still lives here. Get his point of view. See what he has to say for himself. In the morning, I want us to go and have a look at where Smart's clothes were found on the beach. And I know the schools are closed, but we need to speak with any teacher who worked with him.'

'I made some calls after control called me and told me you were coming,' Fletcher said. 'There are two teachers who worked with him still living on the island. One's retired; the other one, not a kick in the pants off it. They'll speak to you tomorrow.'

'Good job. Now, we need a couple of drivers. Robertson, you're driving me and DCI McNeil. Harrison, DCI Dunbar'

'Right. Where are those cars?'

THIRTY-FOUR

Turned out, Susan Robertson had a touch of the Jekyll and Hyde about her when she got behind the wheel of the unmarked car, and Stewart wondered if she was deliberately driving like she was blindfolded to get a boot in at them for daring to come to her wee island and fuck up their cosy existence.

He grabbed the handle above the window and he told her that she could actually follow the rules of the road if she wanted to. It was optional of course. Back in civilisation, most people stopped at a red traffic light, for instance.

'We have to cross over two barrier roads on the way to St Margaret's Hope,' Susan said. 'They're roads that cross the water. Roads that were created.'

'There's no rush,' Stewart said.

'I told them you would be there before dinner.'

'Why did you tell them that? We'll be there when we're there, Constable. What do you say, Harry?'

'Aye, Susan, ease off the welly a bit there. I've got a young daughter back home who I'd like to see again.'

Susan giggled.

Stewart looked round at Harry and made an 'O' with his mouth and raised his eyebrows, indicating the young woman was a nutcase. Then he faced forward again.

'How well do you know the family?' Harry said when Stewart fell quiet.

'Not at all. It's just the parents now. I don't know much about the case. The boys back at the station were going through it. It happened when I was a little girl and people talked about it for years.'

'How far away is this St Margaret's Hope?' Stewart asked.

'About fifteen miles from Kirkwall,' Susan said, smiling at him.

They drove through the darkness, the lights picking out fields on either side of the road. A rig lay out in the water, lit up like a Christmas tree.

Finally, they entered the small town on the coast,

and Susan drove into a street called Front Road and stopped outside a craft workshop.

'It's that one there with the red door,' she said. 'They're expecting you, so just knock. I can wait here if you prefer?'

Stewart looked at her. 'Maybe you could come with us, being a local. They're more likely to open up if one of theirs is there.'

'As you wish.' She turned the engine off and they got out into a gale whipping off the sea at the end of the street.

'First thing we need to do if we ever find this teacher is boot him up the arse,' Stewart said to Harry. 'Putting us through this.'

'I'll be second in line.'

Susan's smile had gone now and she stood looking at the two detectives.

Harry shook his head. 'Metaphorically,' he assured her.

Susan knocked on the front door. There wasn't any pavement to brag about, so they kept their eyes open for anybody who had the same driving skills as Susan, who seemed to have picked hers up from playing *Mario Kart*.

There was an old Ford Focus parked outside the house, so there was a fair chance somebody was in.

Harry and Stewart stood back a bit from Susan, waiting for somebody to open the door. For people who were expecting visitors, they weren't trying to win a gold medal for running up the lobby anytime soon.

Finally, the door opened, just a crack, and a man spoke. 'Who is it?' he asked.

'It's me, Mr Patterson, DC Robertson.'

She made her name sound like a Scottish rapper.

'Right. Hold on.' The door closed and they could hear the noise of a chain sliding along its track.

'Does everybody here act like Michael Myers is going to show up?' Stewart asked.

'I'm not sure,' Susan said. 'I know I do. Put a chain on, I mean.'

The door opened and a man stood before them. He looked like a tramp who'd broken into the house and was trying to pass himself off as the owner. Stubble on his face, unkempt hair and wearing a sweater that looked like he'd whipped it off a corpse that had been in the river, Morris Patterson stepped back and let them in.

Stewart led the way followed by Susan, with Harry trailing behind. It was warm in the house, to the point where it would make ice cream melt in a minute, fighting the cold wind that came in uninvited from the North Sea.

'Go in there,' Patterson said, giving no indication of where to go. The one door that was open had sound coming from beyond it, from a TV, so Stewart went in there.

A woman sat on a chair, facing the box. She looked a lot younger than Patterson, and Stewart wasn't sure if this was actually his wife or not. Her hair was blonde, she was dressed more smartly than Patterson and she looked like she took care of herself.

She slowly looked round. 'Mrs Patterson,' Susan said, stepping forward. 'These are the gentlemen I told you about on the phone.'

Ruby Patterson looked mystified for a moment, as if she couldn't remember any such conversation, but then she smiled, the smile of somebody at a funeral who offers condolences and thanks God that their own loved one is safe back home.

She stood up out of her chair and looked at Stewart and Harry like they were rent men here to collect the TV because she and her husband were behind in the payments.

'Would you like a seat?' she said.

Harry looked at Stewart, who nodded.

'That would be fine,' Harry said, and he and

Stewart sat on the couch, but not next to each other. Stewart always wanted elbow room, so he didn't feel like he was being pickpocketed.

'Anybody for a tea?' Patterson said.

'That would be great,' Susan said. 'Let me help you.' They left the room and headed for wherever the kitchen was.

'She's a nice girl,' Ruby said. 'She lives down here. It's a very quiet place. Not the sort of place you would imagine a murder taking place.' She looked at Harry and Stewart as if expecting one of them to ask who'd been murdered.

But of course they knew it was her daughter. In this very house. Stewart didn't think he could live in a house if his daughter had been murdered in it. He'd probably torch it.

'She is nice, yes,' Harry said. 'She told you we were coming to speak to you about Octavia.'

Ruby's lips were closed and she sucked in a breath through her nose, held it there for a second like this was a rehearsed move to calm herself down, then let the air out again. 'Go ahead, ask away.'

Harry had spoken with Stewart before they left the office and they'd agreed that Harry would start the talking off.

'This is a cold case, as you know, since Angus

Smart was just a suspect and it was believed he committed suicide.'

'You know he was sleeping with her?' Ruby asked, like she'd only just found this out herself.

'It was in the report, yes.'

'Filthy bastard. He was her teacher. Did you know that too?'

'Yes. Have you any idea how long the affair had been going on?'

Ruby made a noise. 'I should have known. Should have seen the signs, but there was nothing. Trust me, I've gone over everything in my head ever since. She never talked about Angus, not once. She was in the drama club after school like others in her class, and I mean, it's not as if she was twelve, she was a consenting adult, but Smart took full advantage of that.'

Stewart looked at her. 'Why do *you* think he killed her?'

'I have no idea. I didn't know anything about the affair. I only knew him as one of Octavia's teachers. You can never tell, though. He seemed nice on the outside, but inside he was a raving psychopath.'

'Sometimes these sorts of crimes are crimes of passion,' Harry said. 'Maybe he got jealous or something. I mean, she would have been surrounded by other boys in school. Maybe he saw this and it put him over the edge.'

'You'd have to ask him that,' Ruby replied. 'Oh, wait, you can't. He's "dead".' Using finger quotes for the last part.

'Don't you believe he's dead?' Stewart asked.

'I would have been happier if he'd hanged himself. Something that everybody could see. Something tangible. But this walking into the sea.' She shook her head. 'Remember John Stonehouse, the MP? He faked his own death, way back in nineteen seventy-four.'

'I remember reading about it years ago,' Harry said.

'What's to say Smart didn't do the same thing? I tried to get them to look into that aspect in more detail, but nobody would listen. Except the detectives who came up from Glasgow to oversee things.'

'Davie Ross and Lynn McKenzie,' Stewart said.

'Aye, that's them. They didn't achieve much in the end. Do you know them?'

'We do. That's why we've come up here, Mrs Patterson,' Harry said. 'You see, two men have been murdered in Edinburgh. There have been similarities to Octavia's murder.'

Her eyes went wide. 'You think it was Angus

Smart?' Her voice was scratchy now, like she couldn't quite compute what she was being told.

'We're not sure. But we'd like a look at Octavia's room, if you don't mind.'

Patterson was just coming in with a tray with some mismatched mugs on it. Stewart could see a plate with a mixture of biscuits on it. The Jammie Dodgers were on the top level.

'I know it's getting close to dinnertime, but there's always room for a cup of tea and a Jammie Dodger,' Patterson said.

'Morris, sweetheart, they want to go and look at Octavia's room.'

'I know they do!' Patterson suddenly shouted, lifting the tray higher before slamming it down onto the floor with a crash. The mugs danced in the air for a second, twirling around with the biscuits, before they landed, two of them colliding and breaking. The biscuits scattered over the carpet, a couple of them rolling away like they were making a run for it.

'Help your-fucking-self!' he screamed, spit coming out of his mouth.

Ruby had jumped up when the tray went crashing, just as Harry and Stewart had, not yet realising the mugs were empty. Susan was behind with the teapot and was looking wildly around her, wondering what to do with the teapot, then she figured it was best to just retrace her steps back to the kitchen.

'Morris!' Ruby screamed.

Susan must have hot-footed it as she was back in a flash, just in time to see the other two detectives climbing back off the settee.

'Why don't you tell them?' Patterson screamed.

'Tell us what?' Stewart said.

'Nothing,' Ruby said, glaring at her husband.

'Why don't you tell them that *you* were fucking Angus Smart too?'

'I told you back then, it was nothing. I wasn't sleeping with him. I met him a few times, that's all.'

'Yeah, right. It was nothing.' Morris made a face like he'd only just discovered there was a poker up his arse.

'Let's everybody calm down,' Susan said.

'It's important that we see Octavia's room, Mrs Patterson,' Harry said. It was important to get at least *her* permission.

'Go ahead,' she said. 'Upstairs, along the landing, second door. You can't miss it; it's the one that looks like a museum.'

'Don't say that!' Morris spat. 'At least you've still got your two.'

Then his shoulders sagged and he let Susan lead him into the kitchen with an arm around his shoulders.

If hate had married revulsion and they'd had a child, this was what was plastered on Ruby's face now. Harry could see their marriage had ended a long time ago and he wondered why they even stayed together anymore.

He and Stewart left the living room and climbed the narrow staircase and went past the bathroom and stood outside the bedroom door with a nameplate on it. *Octavia* was surrounded by flowers.

'It would have been just as easy to tell us to look for the door with her name on it,' Stewart said.

'Grief does funny things, I suppose,' Harry answered and turned the handle. He took a step forward and then stopped, Stewart bumping into him.

'Wee bit of warning before you jam the brakes on, Harry, son,' he said, backing off.

'I can't believe it.'

'What is it?'

'Before you come in, I want to show you something.' Harry took his phone out and opened the photos. The first one was a selfie he'd taken kissing Alex at Glasgow Airport.

'You should really keep that filth to yourself.'

'No, no, wait.' Harry swiped back through some photos until he came to the one he was looking for. 'There, what do you see?'

'A photo of a bedroom.'

'Now look in here.' Harry walked in and Stewart followed. He looked puzzled, then he looked at Harry. 'You didn't take that photo just now, did you?'

'That photo is of the Edinburgh crime scene.'

'What? Let me see that photo again.'

Harry handed over his phone and Stewart held it up with the photo opened. The resemblance was startling: the bed was the same, the side table was the same, even the posters on the wall were the same. Curtains too. The bedspread was the same design, with flowers on it.

'It's like somebody recreated this bedroom in that house you told me about. Jesus.' Stewart looked at Harry as he handed his phone back. 'This guy Tom Powers, he obviously knows what this room looked like.'

'Exactly. He's been here.'

'And we know that there's a good possibility that Angus Smart was in here...'

They were suddenly aware that somebody was behind them. Ruby.

'...playing cards or something,' Stewart said, finishing his sentence.

'You can see he keeps his daughter's room like a shrine to her,' Ruby said.

'*His* daughter?' Harry said.

'Yes. Octavia was my stepdaughter. I have two sons from my first marriage. They were all young when Morris and I met. We'd been married for five years when it happened.'

'Do your sons still live at home?' Harry asked.

Ruby shook her head. 'No. Roger's the oldest.' Her eyes glazed over for a second. 'Daniel's the youngest. Roger started as an apprentice butcher, but he was just biding his time, waiting for Daniel to finish school. Thick as thieves they were. As soon as Daniel was done, the two of them packed up and moved to Glasgow. They stayed there for years. They got themselves into a little bit of trouble, but then they moved to Edinburgh and things settled down for them through there.'

'And they're still there now?' Harry asked.

'As far as I know. I haven't heard from them in a while. They lead busy lives, but I get an email now and again.'

'The murder must have hit them hard,' Stewart said.

'Like you wouldn't believe.'

'Why don't we go back downstairs and you can tell us all about that night, Mrs Patterson,' Harry said. 'We'll meet you down there in a few minutes after we've had a look around.'

'Okay.' She turned away and stopped. Turned to look at them. 'Morris doesn't like anything to be touched. He dusts in there every day.'

'We won't touch anything,' Harry said.

Once she was back down the stairs, he pulled on a pair of sterile gloves. Stewart followed suit.

'Don't touch anything my arse,' Stewart said, picking up a knickknack, looking at it and putting it down in the same spot. Or close to it. 'Typical lassie's room,' he said. 'My Carrie's room was like this, all posters of pop stars with lipstick on them.'

'Who were the pop stars?' Harry asked.

'Don't ask like that.'

'Like what?'

'Like it was fucking Glenn Miller. I know I'm older than you, son, but not by that much.'

Harry smiled. 'I still have that to come.'

'Aye, your wee lassie will be grown up before you know it.'

Harry moved round to the other side of the single bed. It had a wooden headboard and a pink duvet. 'I wonder why the killer would get the same kind of duvet as the one that was on the bed the night she was murdered?'

'Maybe they had two,' Stewart said, opening the louvred doors to the wardrobe. It was a built-in affair, and Octavia's clothes were still hanging in there. He swiped the clothes from one side to the other and put his hand into the pockets of a couple of raincoats and found nothing. But inside the school blazer pocket, he found a piece of paper. He took it out and read it.

Jelly Bean and Octavia sitting in a tree, K-I-S-S-I-N-G.

He read it out to Harry. 'Who's fucking Jelly Bean, I wonder?'

'Some wee snot at school, probably.'

'Aye, but usually when somebody writes that down, it's to torment somebody. Or tease them. Whatever. But the person on the receiving end doesn't usually end up with the paper.'

'True.' Harry was looking through some drawers and stopped to look at Stewart. 'You think she was being bullied?'

'Could be. In any case this piece of paper should

have been submitted into evidence.' Stewart took out a poly bag from his jacket and popped the note in.

There were books on the shelves, including school notebooks. All sorts of subjects. Harry looked through them and stopped at one in particular.

'Here, get this,' he said, pulling the notebook from the shelf.

'What is it?' Stewart asked.

'It's a children's book, written by Octavia. Titled *Jelly Bean and the Beautiful Princess.*'

'Jelly Bean. That was obviously a schoolboy's nickname. We should ask her nibs downstairs if she knows who Jelly Bean is.'

'Listen to this.' Harry started reading out loud. '*Once upon a time there lived a beautiful princess on a lonely island. Every day, she dreamed of meeting a prince who would take her off the island and take her far away, to the Land of Enchantment. She waited and waited for her prince to come, but each day passed and nobody came. She was just beginning to think he would never come when one day a young man appeared in her courtyard. He was a jester and he wanted to make everybody laugh. His name was Jelly Bean.*

'*The king laughed at Jelly Bean and was endlessly amused. So did the princess. She started to have feel-*

ings for Jelly Bean, but just as she thought she was going to marry him, a knight in shining armour came riding into the courtyard. He was on a magnificent horse. It was black and had a beautiful mane. The knight took his helmet off and looked over at the princess. It was love at first sight. She knew then that this knight had to be her husband.

'*The king wasn't pleased about the match, however, because he had already given his word to the jester that he could marry the princess. The princess was heartbroken, and she began to see the knight behind the king's back. Jelly Bean saw them together and got very angry, threatening to tell the king. The knight said he would take her away from this; they would leave the next day. Jelly Bean overheard them and was going to tell the king.*'

Stewart stood looking at Harry. 'Well?'

'That's it. It doesn't seem to be finished. I'm sure that Jelly Bean was Octavia's boyfriend, and he got wind of the affair between Octavia and Angus Smart.'

'It's like she was writing a diary but made it into a children's book instead, in case some old snoopy-drawers came raking about in here,' Stewart said. 'I wonder if Smart knew about Jelly Bean? Maybe like Mrs Patterson said, maybe he was a psycho and he let her have it. He wasn't going to play second fiddle to some daft wee school laddie.'

'That would make sense,' Harry said, taking photos of the pages before putting the notebook back.

'We should go down and have a word with the missus,' Stewart said.

They left the bedroom and went back down. They could hear Susan doing her best to talk softly to old Morris Patterson, presumably in the kitchen. They found Ruby Patterson in the living room, sitting cross-legged, smoking a cigarette.

'He doesn't like me smoking, so I do it to annoy him. Why not? We're finished now anyway.'

The two men stood looking at her.

'Who's Jelly Bean?' Stewart said bluntly, not in the mood for niceties anymore.

'Who? Jelly Bean? Is he on the TV?'

'Come on now, I think you know full well who Jelly Bean is.'

More smoking, like she was determined to turn the wallpaper yellow before she and her husband parted ways. 'He was one of her friends at school.'

'Which one?' Harry said.

Ruby held their gaze for a moment. 'Jelly Bean is Kenny Smith. Your murder victim.'

Stewart looked at Harry before looking back at the woman. 'What about Billy Ferguson?'

Ruby didn't know about Ferguson being murdered and it was kept that way.

'Billy? Is he the other murder victim?' She sucked in her breath and held it for a moment.

'We can't confirm that just yet. Tests have to be done,' Stewart said.

'Billy was such a nice laddie. He was one of her better boyfriends. I liked him.' More blowing smoke. She looked Stewart in the eyes. 'So did Octavia. That was her problem: she liked boys. A lot of them. But can you blame lassies on this island? I mean, there's hardly an abundance of men. So she wasn't just seeing Angus Smart; she was seeing the two boys. That's what I heard. Kenny and Billy. That should all be in the report. They were interviewed after all. The police even got DNA from her bedroom, and nothing happened because they were all her boyfriend at one time, probably at the same time, and I confirmed that yes, they had indeed been in the house and in her bedroom, so of course their DNA was going to be there!'

The two detectives sat down again.

'How long had she known these boys before she died?' Harry asked.

'They went to school together. They saw her every day. They came here, sometimes two at a time, and I thought they were doing homework. Maybe they were. If they were fooling around, then they were doing it while Morris and I were at work.'

'You're sure you gave these names to the original enquiry team?' Stewart asked.

'Of course I did. Those two Glasgow detectives interviewed the boys of course, but they weren't arrested. And as for finding Angus Smart, well, we all know he was smuggled off the island by his brother in that ratty motorhome he has.'

'We have officers interviewing his brother now,' Harry said.

'And you'll all leave again, and still my Octavia's murder will be unsolved. Maybe if you catch whoever killed Jelly Bean, he'll tell you who killed Octavia.'

'Why would he know?' Stewart said.

'I have no idea. I mean, nobody else seems to know.'

Susan came into the living room. 'Mr Patterson's away to the bathroom,' she said, sitting on a chair across from Ruby.

'Where's the lamp?' Stewart asked Ruby. 'The

one that was in Octavia's room when she was murdered.'

'That old thing? It was my mother's. The forensics team took it away and we never saw it again.'

They all heard the front door close. It was just a click, like how a young boy sneaking out late at night might close the door.

Stewart and Harry were on their feet as they heard an engine start outside the house and a car take off.

'Patterson! You up there?' Stewart called, rushing into the hall. He started making his way up the stairs, but he could see the bathroom door was wide open and the room was in darkness. He jumped back down again.

'Where's your husband gone?' he asked Ruby.

She stood up suddenly, like she'd discovered she was on fire. 'Why? What's happened?' She tossed her cigarette into the fireplace.

'You have a car, don't you?'

'Yes, of course. We keep the keys on the kitchen counter in a little basket.'

Stewart and Harry walked quickly through the kitchen, followed by the women. They saw a basket with only one set of keys in it.

'What kind of car do you have?' Harry asked.

'A Ford Focus. Its's parked outside.'

'Not anymore,' Susan said, looking out the window.

'Where would he go?' Stewart asked.

'There's only one place,' Ruby said.

THIRTY-FIVE

Neil and Norma McGovern had been looking forward to spending time with their daughter and two granddaughters.

'I haven't been to the museum in a very long time,' McGovern said.

'Now I'm retired, it's nice to spend more time with the girls,' Norma said. 'I don't miss that place at all,' she added, making a face as she nodded towards the procurator fiscal's office opposite the entrance to the museum on Chamber's Street.

They went in the basement door to the right of the steps, this giving easier access for young Annie.

'I remember you bringing me here, Dad,' Kim said. 'It was like some magical place.'

'I'm glad you have fond memories of it,' McGovern answered.

'Then we got to see the museums in London when we moved down there. They were great too, but I'm glad we moved back home.'

'How's Eric doing these days?' Norma said. Eric was Kim's first husband and the father of Emma, who was holding on tight to Grandpa's hand.

'He's doing well. He's thinking of calling it a day with the army when his time's up.'

'How do you think he'll handle civvy street after being in the SAS?' McGovern said.

'He can adapt.'

'I'm sure he can.'

They walked over to the lift and entered. It had glass walls and gave great views down into the main hall, which was all narrow steel columns and marble floors.

'Can we go to the café afterwards, Grandpa?' Emma asked.

'Of course we can, sweetheart.'

They got out of the lift and headed over to the doors leading into the exhibition. They were a bit early, but one of the curators said it was okay to go in as it wasn't too busy.

The entrance to the *Dr Who* exhibition was through doors that had been made to look like the front of the Tardis. Inside, the girls were excited by the displays, especially Emma, who wanted to see the robot dog, K9.

'Look, they've even put a wee tartan collar on him,' Norma said to the girls.

'Oh, yeah,' Emma said, showing Annie.

They walked over to a display featuring the Half-Face Man next to a robot's head. Norma looked at the man's head. He was aptly named, with the left-hand side of his face gone and a left eye sticking out.

'That looks just like your father after he's been out on a Friday night with his pals,' Norma said, and Kim laughed.

'You're hilarious,' McGovern said but smiled along with them.

They walked past more robots, and a Dalek voice simulator. McGovern walked up to it and spoke into the recorder. 'This is a robbery. Give me all your money!'

A couple turned round to look at him, the young man's eyes going wide.

'No, it's okay, son. I'm just playing with this.' McGovern hit the replay button and the Dalek voice repeated what he had just said.

'Try not to touch stuff, Neil,' Norma said, shaking her head. McGovern shrugged and walked away.

Round the corner, they met with some life-size Daleks and Weeping Angels, creepy statues that belonged in a cemetery.

The girls had fun, playing with some of the exhibits, and then they were in the gift shop.

'That must take some doing, setting all this stuff up,' McGovern said.

'It's like any job; it gets easier over time,' Kim said.

'Look, there's your hero, Norma,' McGovern said to his wife. 'A life-size cut-out of David Tennant, the tenth doctor.'

'He's great, but my favourite was Tom Baker, with his long, colourful scarf.'

'You should get the cut-out. Maybe if you asked him nicely, he would do the dishes,' McGovern said, laughing.

'That's why I keep you around,' Norma chided.

McGovern looked over at their daughter. 'What's wrong, honey?' he said to Kim.

She stared off into space for a moment, then looked at him. 'What? Oh, nothing. Just something Frank said.'

They bought a few gifts for the girls to put in their keepsake boxes, then they went to find the café.

THIRTY-SIX

'What would you call this place?' Angie Fisher said as the headlights cut through the darkness. Jimmy Dunbar was at the wheel, despite his complaining about his eyesight not being as good as it was. A Land Rover overtook him and the driver blasted the horn, which only served to rev Dunbar up, and he leaned on the horn in response.

'I don't care how many fuckers there are in that shitey thing, if he stops and they all bail out wanting a pagger, the three of us are going to show them what it's like to fuck with Glasgow people and no' a bunch of people from the kitting club. You with me?'

'Fuck, yeah,' Angie said. 'Ooh, I'm up for a real pagger. How about you, sweet boy?'

Evans had been a boxer once upon a time and

the chance to go boxing again seemed to perk him up. 'Count me in.'

Dunbar was doing the speed limit, but that hadn't seemed to please the other driver. They saw lights from a house in the distance, and the red tail-lights and now brake lights turn into the driveway of the house.

Dunbar slowed down even more as they passed the modern bungalow. He wound the window down. 'You want to watch your fucking speed!' he shouted to the young man who was getting out of the SUV.

'Is that right, Grandpa?' he said.

Dunbar jumped on the brakes so hard, Angie nearly left her teeth in the dash.

'Aye, it is fucking right.'

The man walked down his drive, all piss and wind. 'And just what the fuck do you think you're going to do about it?'

Evans pulled the door handle, but Angie turned to look at him. 'Leave this to me, pal.' She smiled as she opened her door and walked round the front of the car and strode quickly across to the man, bringing her warrant card out.

'You heard the man: watch your fucking speed. You need to know something, fuck face. I have a younger detective in the back there who would fucking eat you for breakfast. And we're not from around here, and we know how you turnip farmers like to sort things out yourself. Fine by us. Where we come from, we *really* know how to fuck wankers like you over.' Her eyes were blazing and spittle was flying out of her mouth now. 'You want to have a fucking go, I don't even think I'll need the laddie in there. I'll boot your fucking baws right over the back of your shit-faced head. Then Grandpa and the young 'un will make you fucking disappear. You chose the wrong fuck to honk the horn at.'

The man – six feet but skinny and looking like he could be intimidating at a children's birthday party – nodded.

'It's been a long day. Sorry.'

'Go in the house and learn a lesson: be careful who you honk your horn at next time.'

He nodded sheepishly, turned away and walked back up his lit driveway, not looking back.

Angie walked back to the car and got in. 'Sorted,' she said with a smile. 'I was rather hoping he'd take a swing at me, to be honest. I feel like some exercise, and there's nobody to knock out. He came close.'

Dunbar chuckled as he wound up the window. Angie and Evans buckled themselves back in.

'That was impressive, ma'am,' Evans said.

'It was nothing. I've dealt with worse on a Saturday night.'

'Right, Robbie, get your phone out again. I'm lost,' Dunbar said as he pulled away again.

'Carry on up here, left at the T-junction, carry on, then you'll see –'

'Right, Robbie, Christ,' Dunbar said. 'Angie, you're driving back. There's fuck all out here except darkness.'

'Turn the headlights on, boss,' Evans suggested.

'You're funny. All this "I can't drive in case I'm sick" is a load of pish. I don't care if you puke all over the steering wheel, next time you're driving.'

'You just said DCI Fisher is driving back.'

'Not tonight. Pay attention.' Dunbar brought the car to a stop. 'Which way? Left or right?'

'I already told you left.' Evans tutted.

'Now, now, boys.' Angie smiled at Dunbar in the darkness. 'You wonder why we women give you directions? Because we're always right.'

Dunbar opened his mouth to argue, but then thought better of it and closed it again. He turned left and carried on down the road. Evans gave him directions in a voice that was louder than strictly necessary.

'It should be around here somewhere,' Evans

said. 'I was going to say, slow down, but we're just about crawling as it is.'

'Shut your hole. There it is. That farmhouse on the left.'

Surprisingly, there were lights on around the yard, and a light on above the door to the farmhouse itself. An old metal shed that was big enough to fit farm vehicles lay further back.

The headlights swept across the front of the stone house and Dunbar pulled the car to a stop near a Toyota pickup truck that had seen better days.

'Maybe better put the torch on,' Evans said, playing with his phone until the little light on the back came on, illuminating the back of the car. 'Don't want to stand in cow shite.'

'Or dog shite,' Angie added.

'Preferably no' any kind of shite,' Dunbar said, getting his own light on.

They got out of the car and walked up to the front door and knocked.

A scraggy man answered. He was wearing an old tweed jacket over a sweater that had a hole in it, items of clothing that a tramp would tell somebody to shove up their arse if they were offered to him.

'We're looking for Rory Smart,' Evans said. 'Is he in?'

'I'm Rory Smart,' the man replied.

Evans gave him a look that suggested he thought the man had been one gene away from ending up in a jar in the university.

'Really?'

'Aye. How were you expecting me to answer the door? In my tux?'

'Can we come in?' Dunbar asked, shooting Evans a look.

'I was wondering when you cu...people would show up,' Rory said. 'Ma'am,' he said, doffing an imaginary cap when he saw Angie. 'Come in, you're making the fucking house freezing.'

He walked back along the hallway.

'I bet he has a scarecrow that dresses better than he does,' Evans whispered.

'Shut up and get in,' Dunbar said, giving the younger detective a shove.

They trooped in and could hear a dog barking from another room.

'Angus! Shut your piehole.'

Evans looked at Dunbar and Angie and raised his eyebrows; the dog had the same name as Rory's brother, Angus.

The living room was worse than a cowp, a smelly, filthy hovel that made you glad you had been given some sort of vaccination when you were a child. This place left minging well behind in the race to be the smelliest bastard place on earth.

'Have a seat if you want. I'd better let Angus out or else he'll chew the dining table leg again.'

The Jack Russell terrier came booting into the living room at full tilt, leaped up onto the manky settee, up onto the back of it, and stopped as if he had only just realised they had company. He started yapping at them.

'Angus! Go to your bed.'

The little dog jumped down and went to his dog bed in the corner, where he chewed on a toy but kept his eyes peeled in case he was called into action to sort out one of the newcomers. Ankles, hands or bollocks, he wasn't fussy what part of the anatomy he latched on to.

Dunbar, Evans and Angie stood around, trying not to breathe through their noses.

'I heard about you drudging Angus's name up again, so come on, let's have it. What do you want to know this time? Been another murder in Glasgow that you could maybe pin on my brother?'

'No, nothing like that,' Angie said.

'Sorry, love, but I'd rather speak to the boss, if you don't mind.'

Dunbar winced and Evans lifted his eyebrows in an 'oh no you didn't' way.

Dunbar noticed a slight shift in Angie's stance, a subtle movement that you wouldn't see if you didn't know what to look for.

'Never been married, have you, Rory?' she asked him.

'Nope. Read that in your boss's report, did you?'

'Not quite. I guessed it in the first few seconds. I have a nose for that sort of thing,' she said. 'Ignorant tossers who have lived their whole lives thinking women are inferior. Like you still live in the nineteen fifties.'

'Are you going to stand there and let her talk to me like that?' Rory said to Dunbar.

'She's the same rank as me, pal: DCI. As far as I'm concerned, she can talk to anybody any way she wants.'

'Christ, what sort of world do we live in?' Rory tutted and shook his head. 'Anyway, what do you want to know about Angus?' The dog raised his head and looked at him. 'Not you.' He went back to chewing his toy.

'You can start by telling us where he is,' Angie said.

'I was hoping you could tell me.'

'We've read the reports from back then, Rory: the fake suicide, trying to throw the polis off the scent after he allegedly killed the girl.'

Rory laughed. 'You think you've got it all sewn up, don't you? Come back here after twenty-three years and think I'll have changed my mind? Well, I can't change my mind because I don't know where he is. Why now, after all this time?'

'Two of the boys who lived here around the time of the murder have been found murdered themselves, in Edinburgh.'

'Jesus.' Rory looked at what passed for a carpet for a few seconds as if trying to spot a clean patch, somewhere the dog hadn't pissed on, or where a baked bean hadn't scooted off the plate onto the floor. He had mentioned a dining table that the dog chewed on, but Dunbar reckoned this room was where the older man ate his meals. A folding TV tray table sat against the wall near the TV with a red stain on it; either ketchup or he'd recently battered somebody with it.

'Who would want to kill them?' he asked nobody in particular. The dog stopped chewing for a second, like he was going to weigh in, but then went back to chewing. 'And who died?'

'We were thinking that maybe Angus had caught

up with them. Maybe bumped into them and things got out of hand and he killed them,' Dunbar said.

Rory laughed, but it was more of a guttural sound, a short laugh of disbelief. 'Angus? You've got to be kidding me. And I asked you who it was.'

'Kenny Smith and Billy Ferguson,' Angie said.

Rory's head snapped towards her. 'Kenny and Billy? Christ, Angus taught them at school. He was one of their teachers.'

'Somebody murdered them in a very specific way, Mr Smart,' Dunbar said. 'We need to know why somebody would want to kill them and whether it was connected to your brother's disappearance.'

'Suicide,' Rory corrected them. 'Angus was guilty of nothing more than falling in love with the wrong woman. Aye, she was only a lassie, but she was technically a woman. They were going to run away together to the mainland.'

'Did you take him to the mainland?' Dunbar asked.

Rory's shoulders slumped and once again he looked for any signs that the pattern on the carpet had actually once existed. Then he made eye contact with Dunbar. 'I was going to drive the two of them to the mainland. We were going to leave on the Saturday morning on the first ferry. They were going to do it then because her mother and father were away for a few days visiting somebody. She was going to leave with him, then they would hide in the motorhome I have, so they wouldn't be registered on the ferry.'

'You ended up just taking Angus?' Dunbar said.

'Hand on my heart, he never showed up. People thought the clothes on the beach was a poor attempt to take the heat off himself by making people think he'd walked into the sea, but believe me, if I had thought he was guilty of murdering that lassie, I would have handed over the wee bastard myself. But he never came near here. The last time I heard from him was when he called me to say he was going to meet Octavia at a park. Later on, when I hadn't heard from him, I called him, but there was no answer. I never heard from him again.

'Then a couple of days later, the police came knocking. I let them search everywhere and I was interrogated. By some nasty bastard from Glasgow and his sidekick, a young woman. Younger than you,' he said to Angie, nodding at her. 'I can't remember their names now, of course, but they were a pair of tough bastards. They got nowhere with me, though, because I told them the truth. I didn't know where he was. They checked with the ferry company and saw that I had a ticket booked but it wasn't used. I had been going to see a pal of mine on the mainland but cancelled.'

'Have you any theories about where he went to?' Dunbar said. 'I mean, you're an intelligent man; do you think he really walked into the water?'

Rory took in a deep breath and let it out. 'No. I swear to God I don't know where he went, but Angus wouldn't have been that stupid.' He paused. 'Look, I'm going to tell you something that I didn't tell those other Glasgow coppers. I mean, I might have if they hadn't come storming in here like they owned the fucking place.'

He shook his head. 'Listen. I lied, ok? I *did* hear from him. After he said he was waiting for her...'

Back then

Angus Smart got in his car and looked for any blues cutting through the darkness, but there were none. He cracked the window a bit, listening for sirens. Again, none.

He took his phone out and looked up a contact.

'*That you two ready then?*' Angus's brother, Rory, said on the other end.

'Rory, something bad's happened!'

'*Oh God, has she changed her mind? I told you that might happen.*'

'It's worse than that. She's dead, Rory!' Angus felt his voice breaking, but he held it together. 'Somebody murdered her. She's lying on her bed, dead. Somebody killed her, Rory, and they're going to think it was me. What am I going to do now? My life's over. I'll go to prison for the rest of my life.'

'*Right, listen to me. Take the road going out of town, heading south...*'

Now

'You were going to be harbouring a killer, then?' Angie said, still rankled at the misogynist's earlier comment.

'I know my own brother. Angus is no killer. He said he found her that way and I believed him. We had talked about him running away with Octavia for a few months. Of course there was Emily to think of.

His live-in girlfriend. She had two kids. Our dad thought he was a fool for moving in with her since she had two mouths to feed, kids that Angus hadn't fathered.'

'Your father still around here?' Dunbar asked.

Rory shook his head. 'The old man's long gone. I still think this thing with Angus sent him to an early grave.'

'What about Emily? Does she still live here?' Evans asked.

'Nope. That whore buggered off to the mainland years ago after her sprogs grew up.'

'Did she think Angus was guilty?' Angie asked.

'Everybody on the island except me and Dad thought he was guilty. There's a different way of looking at things up here. Sometimes we deal with things our way. Angus would have been in front of a kangaroo court.'

'Tell us what happened after Angus called you that night,' Dunbar said.

'I told him to go round the coast road so he could come here. We'd dump his car, and the next morning I'd drive to the mainland in the motorhome. But he never called. I never heard from him again. The next day, I acted normal. I went to the funeral of some old boy who'd died. She hadn't been found by then. The parents were at her mother's house or something like that. The woman was ill, so the kids stayed behind because they weren't really kids anymore. They were staying at their grandfather's house. Anyway, when we were at the funeral for the old boy, somebody shouted me over, saying that they'd found Angus's clothes and wallet on the beach at the Millennium Stone and the police had been called. They were shocked and started firing off a thousand questions: *Was he suicidal? What would make him do it? Blah, blah, blah.* Then Octavia was discovered and they soon knew why Angus had walked into the sea.'

'You said you don't believe that he did that,' Dunbar said.

Rory shook his head. 'Angus wouldn't have been that brave. I mean, I know he was on a hiding to nothing. Who was going to believe he didn't do it except me and Dad? Nobody. They all thought he was nice, but when they learned he was shagging...I mean, sleeping with a student, he was no better than a Nazi. Some of those Neanderthals tried their shite with me, saying I knew, and coming up to the farm like they wanted to burn the place down. My shotgun soon persuaded them not to try anything.'

'You used a weapon to threaten people?' Dunbar said.

Rory nodded. 'Aye.' Simple as that.

Dunbar nodded. 'Fair enough.'

'We know it was a big enquiry that went cold,' Evans said. 'Are you sure you didn't meet up with your brother and take him to the mainland?'

'I'm sure, sonny. I've lived under this cloud for a long time.'

Jimmy Dunbar's phone rang and he looked at the screen. 'I have to take this.' He stepped out of the room for a minute and they heard his voice as he replied to the caller.

He rushed back into the room and looked at Angie and Evans.

Then he looked at Rory. 'That was my colleague on the phone. They think they've found your brother.'

THIRTY-SEVEN

'Susan, you know these roads. Feel free to boot the shite out of this machine,' Stewart said.

Ruby had come running out with them and she opened a back door and jumped in.

'Mrs Patterson, you're going to have to get out of the car,' Harry said. He had already climbed into the back of the polis car in case Stewart had any ideas about asking him to sit in the front with Evel Knievel.

'That'll be right. I think I know where he's going. You two, get in.'

Stewart got into the front passenger seat. Harry looked out of the window, avoiding eye contact. Susan jumped in behind the wheel and all the doors were closed.

'St Peter's,' Ruby said. 'He goes there all the time to speak to Octavia.'

'That's the cemetery, I take it?' Stewart said.

'It is.'

They got belted in as Susan drove with the same skill as drunk drivers and teenage car thieves everywhere; with gusto, wild abandon and the attitude of 'it'll never happen to me'.

Stewart was reminded why he didn't like rollercoasters; that too involved being strapped inside a machine that you had no control over. Despite her best efforts, Susan had lost sight of Patterson, if she'd ever had him in her sights to begin with, which Stewart doubted. Patterson must have been driving like a madman.

When they turned onto the road for the small church and graveyard, they could see a pair of headlights in the distance.

They slowed down on the approach to the churchyard. The car was parked, its headlights still on, the driver's door flung wide open. The lights were shining through the iron gate into the churchyard itself, illuminating Morris Patterson standing by a gravestone.

Susan stopped the car behind Patterson's,

attempting to block him in, in case he thought of jumping in behind the wheel.

'There's a gap at the front of his car between the bumper and the gate. He could just swing his car round if he wants to get away,' Stewart said to Susan as they all bailed out.

'Oh.'

'Ten out of ten for trying.' He looked at Patterson being illuminated by the headlights. 'Let's go and see what old Morris is up to.'

'I know you're upset, Morris, but let's go back home,' Ruby shouted, the wind catching her words and tossing them about like Scrabble tiles in a blender.

Patterson just stood looking at them, making no attempt to run, which pleased Stewart, who wasn't built for running, especially in the dark in a strange place, running after some baldy wee radge who knew the territory.

They all moved through the gate and walked towards Patterson.

'Is this your daughter's grave?' Harry asked.

Ruby shook her head while the wind shook her hair. 'No. Octavia's over there.'

She pointed a finger to the new part of the churchyard.

'Do you know whose grave it is?' Stewart asked.

'That's Bob McArthur. Just one of the locals. His funeral was the day before Octavia was found murdered.'

Stewart looked at Patterson, at his watery eyes, and saw nothing inside.

'This island has secrets,' Patterson shouted. 'Sometimes people do bad things, and they're taken care of the old-fashioned way.'

'Shut up, Morris!' Ruby said, but it was clear that her husband wasn't ready to shut up.

'I'm sick of this eating away at me, eating away at my very being. Do you know, I still jump whenever somebody knocks on the door or rings the doorbell. Why? Because I think they've come to take me away. When the detective from Edinburgh said they were looking into the cold case, I felt the panic rising inside again. Every single time that damn doorbell went. Well, no more. I'm sick of living like this.'

'What are you talking about?'

Just then, another car's headlights came down the narrow road, and Jimmy Dunbar got out the front of the car. Angie was driving and there were two other people in the back; Evans and another man stepped out from the back and they all walked over to the gate.

'You may as well hear it from me, Rory,' Patterson shouted. 'I killed your brother. The night of the murder. I followed him here. He thought it was the police. That's what he told me. I said, did you see any blue flashing lights?' Patterson shook his head. 'I told him I'd seen him coming out of my house. I only came back to check on the kids, even though they weren't really kids, but my dad, their grandpa, was looking after them and I really wanted to see that he was okay. But as I was passing the house, I saw Angus leave. I'd heard a rumour about them, him and my Octavia, but I didn't want to believe it. I was going to confront her, but I didn't want to lose her. She was all I ever cared about. What could I have done that wouldn't drive her away? So I did nothing. Until it was too late.'

'What about me?' Ruby screamed. 'I should have been number one!'

'Like *I* should have been. Not your boys! Me!'

'They're my children!'

'Just like Octavia was mine!'

'What happened when you caught up with Angus?' Stewart asked.

'Well, boys of her own age fooling around with her was one thing, but to have a teacher doing that? No, I wasn't having that.' Patterson reached behind

295

the gravestone and pulled out the shotgun he'd been hiding.

'Jesus,' Stewart said.

'Don't do anything rash, Morris,' Harry said.

Patterson ignored him. 'No, I wasn't having that. I told him he wasn't going to get away with sleeping with Octavia. And I let him have it. Over this grave. He fell in and I buried him. They were going to bury old man McArthur the following day anyway. I took clothes out of his suitcase and left them on the beach with his wallet. If nobody else went down to the Millennium Stone, I was going to, after the funeral. Just for a few moments of peace. But the lads went down and found the stuff. And of course, Smart's car was already parked here. Nobody knew for sure that he had committed suicide, but there was never any sighting of him. Because he's in there.' He pointed to the grave.

'Did you kill Kenny Smith and Billy Ferguson?' Harry asked. 'In Edinburgh.'

'No, of course not. I've been here the whole time.'

Ruby nodded. 'He has.'

'Then why did somebody kill them?'

'Ask her! Ruby will tell you!'

'Morris, please! It was a long time ago.' She walked closer to her husband.

'Give me the gun, Morris,' Stewart said.

Patterson raised it and pointed it at him. 'Stay away.' Then he swung it towards Ruby. 'Tell them that Octavia wasn't the only one sleeping with Jelly Bean and Whizz.' He laughed. 'Three of them had nicknames from comic book characters in primary school, and they stuck; God knows where Jelly Bean came from. Four lads. Two of them were her sons. The four of them were inseparable, and they were always coming round our house. Then one of them caught Ruby's eye. Jelly Bean, young Kenny Smith himself. Screwing my wife.'

'I'm not your wife, remember!' Ruby shouted. She turned to look at Stewart. 'We never officially married, but I used his name.'

'Why don't you tell them all of it? Or are you scared they'll go and get your boys?' Patterson laughed. 'That daft bitch would watch old black-and-white films with the boys. They lapped it up. They're dafter than she is.'

'Shut up! Leave my boys out of it.'

Morris laughed. 'I killed that bastard in there for sleeping with my daughter.' He pointed to the grave with the shotgun. 'Everybody thought he'd killed my Octavia after she was discovered. Turns out the nut job son did. Helped no doubt by the younger one. I heard them talking on the phone one night, years later. Ruby said that nobody knew and everybody still thought it was Angus Smart. Then she said, "I know you didn't mean to kill her. Just stick with your brother and he'll make sure you're alright." That's right, isn't it, Ruby?'

'I'm saying nothing.'

'Then I heard her talking to one of them again. Talking about how Jelly Bean – Kenny – was going to write a memoir. His pal, Billy, was going to help him. They had a falling-out with her two sons and they said they were going to include a chapter solely about how they both had an affair with their friends' mum. Her right there, the squeaky clean Ruby Patterson.'

'Maybe I should have married Kenny Smith when I had the chance! Yeah, that's right, he wanted to run away with me. I wish I'd taken him up on the offer now.'

'You must be joking. A washed-up old cow like you? Please.'

'Well, maybe I'll just look for a toy boy when you're spending the rest of your life in prison for murder! Yeah, a nice toy boy like Jelly –'

She didn't get to finish the sentence before the shotgun blast cut her short. The entry wound in her chest was the size of an orange at close range and it killed her instantly, throwing her back onto another old grave.

Angie threw herself onto Rory Smart, knocking him to the ground and staying on him to protect him. The other officers ducked and ran for cover. Then they heard a second bang, and Morris Patterson lay on the wet grass just feet from where his dead wife lay. There wasn't much left of his head, most of it having sprayed the surrounding grass and headstones.

The officers and Rory Smart stood back up.

'Jesus,' Rory said, and turned away to be sick behind another gravestone.

Stewart looked at Harry. 'Get onto your team to start a search for her sons. They could be anywhere, maybe even abroad, but if they're still in the UK, I want them found.'

'We don't know their last names,' Harry said.

'But somebody else here does.' Stewart looked at Rory, who was standing up and wiping his mouth with the back of his hand.

'Give me a minute, squire.'

THIRTY-EIGHT

Skellett and Miller were talking at a computer when the phone rang. Elvis and Lillian were at their own desks.

'Hey, boss,' Miller said.

He listened for a few moments as Harry relayed the information. Then he hung up.

'Listen up. There's been a breakthrough on the case in Orkney.' Miller filled them in.

'Elvis, Lilian, I want you both to go to the production centre at Sighthill where they store the evidence. There's one piece of evidence that we're interested in: the lamp that was at the Orkney crime scene. DCI McNeil seems to think that the one that was in the gardener's cottage was the real deal, somehow taken from the production centre. Find out how that could have happened.'

'I know how that could have happened,' Elvis said, looking up from his computer.

'How?' Skellett said, all ears now.

The other three detectives looked at Elvis.

'There are weirdos who buy stuff like that on auction sites. You know, items that were part of a murder. Knives, clothing, sometimes a drawing that a killer drew in prison.'

'People collect that shite?' Skellett said, making a face.

'Yes, they do. It's worth a lot of money to the right buyer.'

'I'm in the wrong game,' Miller said.

'So what if this happened?' Elvis said, carrying on with his theory. 'What if somebody bought the lamp from production? Somebody unscrupulous working there sold it?'

'Elvis, you and I will go and have a talk with somebody there,' Miller said. 'Charlie? Lillian? We have two names to trace. Original natives from Orkney.'

'We'll get right on it, sir,' Lillian said.

Miller and Elvis left the building. Skellett took

his phone out and dialled Julie's number, but there was no answer. It went right to voicemail. 'Julie, it's Charlie. Just checking in. Call me when you get a chance.'

He hung up and hoped she was feeling better. But something nagged away at him.

Sighthill Industrial Estate was on the west side of Edinburgh, nudging up to the bypass. It was a mix of drab buildings that would have given a borstal a run for its money.

'It's been years since I was here,' Miller said.

The tramline ran parallel with the road that led to Hermiston Gate shopping park. Miller felt like he was racing the tram as it took off from the stop at South Gyle Access, then he slowed and turned left, heading to a unit near the top.

'Whoever works here could be working with the killer,' Elvis said.

'Be on your toes,' Miller replied.

He stopped at a two-storey building; the entrance to the warehouse was on the lower half in a different street. This estate was built on hills, so some buildings had different levels on different streets.

Miller and Elvis approached the main door. They were buzzed in by a security guard and they showed their warrant cards.

'You'll have to sign in,' the guard said.

'Are you always on duty up here?' Miller asked.

'Oh, yes. There are others too, of course. We work twenty-four-hour shifts. Same with the warehouse. They're not rotating shifts, though. Night shift does nights and that's it.'

'Who works the later shifts?'

The guard looked at the roster. 'That will be Barney Cheetham and Nigel Keith. They're pulling an extra shift now because a bloke on the day shift is off sick and the other one just left. We can't keep the bloody staff nowadays.'

'Are they downstairs?'

'Yes. You want me to call them?'

'No need. We just want to look at something.'

Miller and Elvis walked through the security door into the main building.

'Lucky for us that lazy bastard called in sick,' Barney Cheetham said to his friend. He was under another rack, pulling out boxes and trying not to suck in dust. 'Nige? You there, mate? Cause I could do with a fucking hand down here.'

'Here, let *me* help you then,' a strange voice said.

Shite. Was this the new manager they'd got wind of? Some daft bastard who wanted to work at the weekend and get a *Blue Peter* badge for his efforts?

Barney shuffled out – still without fucking knee pads! – and got himself onto the warehouse floor with a struggle. His face was red and he straightened up his sweater once he was on his feet.

'Help you?' he said to the stranger. He had to work with plenty of strangers, from coppers to forensics geeks. They were the worst to work with. They thought they knew it all. Bunch of fannies.

'I'm DI Frank Miller. This is my colleague DC Colin Presley.'

'Like the singer?' Barney said, nodding to Elvis.

'Aye, like the singer.'

'Right.' Barney nodded and tucked his shirt in at the back. 'Sup?'

'I'm looking for something,' Miller said. 'An item from a crime scene from twenty-three years ago.'

'Do you have a location number?'

'Nope.'

'We really need a location number. As you can see, there are literally thousands of items in here. I can't help you without it.' Barney pointed to two of the boxes. 'See those there? They're for a team in Wester Hailes. They filled in the form and requested the stuff, and we come and get it out and they send a uniform to fetch it. They didn't just waltz in here and spring something on us. Sorry, but you'll have to go through the proper channels.'

'Is that what your buyer did? Go through the proper channels?'

'What are you talking about, mate?' Barney looked over Miller's shoulder.

'If you're looking for your pal Nigel, he's sitting in the security office with some uniforms. Again, I'll ask you, does your buyer put in an advance notice?'

'*Again*, I know fuck all about what you're talking about.'

Miller took a step closer and got in Barney's face. They were eye to eye now. 'Let me put this to you in the simplest terms, because you seem to be a simpleton. That lamp you sold to your buyer was used at a murder scene. Everything was staged to make it look like another crime scene. The person you sold it to is completely unhinged. He or she could come back for you, because you know too much. Either way, you're going to be charged as an accessory to murder. That carries a minimum of ten years. You and your pal upstairs.'

'Murder? Fuck no, I'm just stealing stuff and selling it. Shite that's been in here for years. Shite that nobody wants or cares about.'

'I care about it!' Miller said, getting right in Barney's face now. 'That stuff is here because we go through old cold cases, trying to solve a murder, and sometimes it just takes looking at a piece of evidence to send us in the right direction. But since you've sold half of it, another murder might never be solved. Do you get that through your fucking thick skull?' Miller poked the man in the forehead before stepping back. He was breathing heavily now.

'If you help me, I can see if we can get the charges downgraded from accessory to murder to theft. That's the only time I'm going to say that. If you tell me to fuck off, I will do just that and the procurator fiscal will be all over you like a fucking rash. And I'll put in a word to Saughton that you had kiddie porn on your computer.'

'Wait, what? Fuck no. You can't do that. That

isn't fair. They'll eat me alive in prison. I'm not built for doing that kind of stuff.'

'Then give me a name in the next twenty seconds or you're out of here.' Miller looked at his watch.

Barney hesitated. Miller just stood looking at his watch. 'Ten seconds and your life is upside down. Nonce.'

'Aw, fuck me. Okay. He said his name was Tom Powers. He wore a beard and a hat and dressed like Dr Who. The one with the long scarf. But I knew him. Not as Tom Powers. He'd been in here before, but not buying stuff for himself. In a work capacity. I recognised the voice. I can't remember his name off-hand, because it's been a long time. But I can look it up.' Barney looked at Miller. 'Please don't say I'm a nonce. I'm just a fucking thief.'

'Your chances are looking better. But you'd better find that name.'

'I will. We'll have to go into the security suite and let me get on a computer.'

They followed Barney upstairs.

Lynn McKenzie had just got off the phone with Calvin Stewart and sat down, preparing herself for an evening of watching an old film on TV and having a glass of wine. Calvin's wine, the stuff he bought to impress her, not knowing it was used as paint stripper in some parts of the world.

She was looking forward to having Calvin back. Never in a million years would she have seen herself being with the man, but now here they were, officially a couple. Lynn got on well with Calvin's family too – his daughter, Carrie, and the wee man, his grandson, Eddie.

Calvin wouldn't be able to get a flight back until early the following morning, but absence did something to the heart and all that, she thought.

Then her phone buzzed. She looked at the text.

Ma'am, we haven't met, but I'm DS Julie Stott. I work with Calvin Stewart. I have information on the case we're working on. I'm scared. This has gone way over my head. Could we meet up?

Lynn's heart skipped a beat as she replied. *I've heard DSup Stewart talk about you. Of course we can meet up. Where are you?*

She held the phone, staring at the screen, waiting for a reply.

I'm at Fettes in the Incident room.

She shot out a quick reply. *I'll be there in five.*

She stood up, put her phone in her pocket and grabbed a jacket on the way out. She locked the door and skipped down the stairs. Outside, it was bitterly cold, and dark and miserable. She had to walk round the corner to where she had parked her car.

Being a police officer, she was always keenly aware of her surroundings, but this time somebody was better than she was.

'Just keep walking and you won't get hurt,' a voice said as a hand grabbed her elbow. 'Believe me, I may look old, but this is all just fake. I could outrun you any day of the week.'

If only Lynn had thought about it; if this man had been the one dressed as Santa who'd attacked Davie, then his knee would still be hurting after getting belted with a bottle. This man wasn't limping. He wasn't the one who'd attacked Davie. He was still dressed as Santa, though.

Who the hell was he? She realised now that Julie hadn't sent the text. Maybe it had come from her phone, but she certainly hadn't sent it.

He led her round to a car and opened a back door. There was somebody else sitting inside. A man with a bushy grey beard, wearing a hat and a multi-coloured scarf.

'You must be the famous Tom Powers,' she said sarcastically. 'I've been waiting to meet you for a long time now.'

'Likewise,' Powers answered.

Santa got in behind the wheel and they drove away.

THIRTY-NINE

Charlie Skellett sat doodling on a pad of paper in front of him, drawing circles, making them into what might have been faces. As it was, he wasn't going to be making a fortune from his art anytime soon.

Lillian came across with a cup of coffee and put it on his desk.

'Thanks, hen,' he said, sitting up straight so he could drink the coffee without spilling it and burning his goolies off.

'Is everything alright, Charlie?' she asked, sitting down at her own desk.

'These names. I've not had one damn hit. Have you?'

'Nothing yet. Dan Jenkins and Roger Jenkins. There are millions of them, but none of them jump out as being psychos. I wish they would make a book, like a phone directory, and just have psychos in it. That would make life easier for us.'

'Wouldn't that be good. Maybe I should write one,' Charlie said, chuckling.

'You know what they say: if it was easy, then everybody would be doing it.' She took a sip of her coffee, then sprayed it over her desk.

'Christ, you alright there?' Charlie asked.

'Dan Jenkins! The two people who found Kenny Smith's body in the gardener's cottage; the guy was called Dan Jenkins.'

'You sure?'

'Look it up. His statement will be in the system.'

Charlie made a face like she had just asked him to juggle three balls while stripping down a car engine at the same time.

'Let me do it.' She wiped at the coffee and started tapping on the keyboard. 'There it is, Dan Jenkins.'

'Do we have an address for him?'

'We do.' More tapping. 'Oh, shite.'

'What is it, Lillian?'

'Obviously, nobody checked his address before they uploaded it into the system. The address he gave is in Longstone.'

'What's wrong with that?'

'It's the bus depot, Charlie.' She shook her head. 'Maybe he told Julie where he lives. She was the one interviewing him in the big house while I interviewed the woman.'

'Julie's sick and she's not answering her phone.'

'Oh Christ, that's all we need.'

'Do you want to tell Calvin Stewart, or will I?'

'Call Lynn McKenzie. At least she tells you you're a useless arsehole in a more upscale accent.'

'Look up her number, will you? I'll give her a bell after I've been to the lav to adjust my brace. That useless doctor wanted to go in there and poke about without any guarantee that it would be fixed. Can you believe that?'

'I'll look it up. Then we can maybe order Chinese or something. I'm starving.'

FORTY

It seemed like the whole of Police Scotland Orkney Division had turned out at the small church. William Williams was front and centre.

'I called Inverness like you asked me to, sir, but they're full.'

'What do you mean, they're full?' Stewart said. 'You did call the polis station and no' the Holiday Inn Express?'

'I did. They said they're up to their "hairy bollocks" in cases.'

'Did they now?' Angie said, stepping forward. 'Give me their number and I'll give the bastards a roasting.'

'Not necessary, ma'am,' Williams said, laughing. 'Although I'd pay money to see that. But Aberdeen are on their way. They won't be here until tomorrow.'

Stewart shook his head. 'Right, that'll have to do.'

Then Stewart's phone rang. 'Hello?'

'Calvin, it's Charlie.'

'Oh, aye, all respect out the fucking window now, is it? I hope you've got your fucking troosers on while you're talking to me.'

'Shut up and listen. Lynn's not answering her phone. Lillian drove over the road to your place and there's nobody answering the door. The next-door neighbour, Myra, said Lynn went out a wee while ago. But her car's still there, Myra says. And get this: she was seen walking along the road with Santa-fuck-ing-Claus.'

'What? Fuck's sake. I told her to stay put. Why the hell did she go out?'

'I can't answer that. But listen. We've got a hit for one of the names, Dan Jenkins. The young guy who was at the big house where Kenny Smith was found. I wasn't there, but Lillian was, and she remembered the name. But we've got hee-haw on the other name. Are you sure about the other one, Roger Jenkins?'

Stewart turned round to Harry. 'Where's fucking Heid-the-Baw?'

'Which one?' Harry asked.

'Rory Smart.'

'Over there,' Harry said, nodding. The place was lit up like a playing field now, with all the headlights.

'Oi! Rory! You sure about the names of those boys?'

Rory ambled over like he was trying not to step in cow shite.

'Aye, I'm sure. They had nicknames for each other. Dan and Roger Jenkins.'

Stewart nodded and looked away. 'Nope,' he said to Skellett. 'You're stuck with those. If that Dan *is* the same one, then I want him brought in.'

'I'm getting hold of the key holder now for the estate agency. These things take time. But I'm more worried about Lynn and Julie.'

'Julie Stott?'

'Aye.'

'What the fuck's wrong with her?'

'I can't get hold of her. She called in sick, and now she's...what's it called again? Ghosting me.'

'Keep trying. I'm going to come back with Harry and Angie.'

'Who?'

'A colleague. Keep trying to get hold of Lynn and Julie. I'll see you in a few hours. Get on to business support and get me three tickets to Edinburgh. And get them to hold the plane. We won't be long.'

'*Will do.*'

Stewart hung up and got his team together. 'Me, Harry and Angie are going home. Lynn McKenzie and Julie Stott – one of my team – are missing. Jimmy? You stay here with Robbie and keep an eye on things until Aberdeen get here. I'm going to have that plane wait on us.' He looked at his watch. 'It will be getting ready now, but they'd bloody well better wait. It's the last one tonight, and it's going to Edinburgh.'

'Right you are, sir,' Evans said.

'And have DCI Dunbar bring our gear home. We're going straight to the airport.'

'Will do.'

'And don't be raking about in my fucking bag. I've got all my cash on me.'

'Like I'm going to touch your manky skids,' Evans said in a low voice.'

'What?'

'Nothing,' Evans said.

'I'm no' fucking deef.' Stewart turned to Susan. 'Right, hen, take us to the airport, and drive it like you just fucking stole it.'

FORTY-ONE

Something had been nagging away at Charlie Skellett and it wasn't the Velcro on his leg brace. It was the name 'Jenkins'. He was sure he'd heard it before, and recently. Somebody in the pub? On the news? *Fuck's sake. Come on, Charlie, ya dundering old bastard.*

'I'm waiting on the key holder to go and open the estate agency and get into their system,' Lillian said for the second time. Or maybe it was the third?

'What's keeping them? Is there a match on TV or something?' Skellett tossed an eraser at the white-board. It missed, proving once again that the darts team had dodged a bullet when he hadn't applied to play.

'That's the plane taken off,' Lillian said, using

some kind of flight tracker on her phone. She'd tried to show Skellett, who had managed to download a fight club app and an application form for a new credit card.

'I have sausage fingers,' he had told Lillian. 'Those wee virtual keyboards weren't for men like me who are well endowed.'

'Unless you're planning on tapping your phone with your willy, I would keep those sorts of remarks to yourself,' Lillian had said.

'I thought that meant you had big fingers?'

'How am I going to know when you've really gone daft when you keep talking like this?'

'Anyway, they're not meant for big fingers, and fine well you know that's what I meant.'

'Aye, I did. I just wanted to see if you'd pull a beamer,' she'd said.

Skellett sat at his desk, pondering. 'Jenkins!' he shouted sitting up so fast in his office chair, he nearly added a back injury to his knee injury. He pulled open his desk drawer and rifled through some papers, tossing them onto his desk until he found the one he wanted.

'Found it, ya bastard. Look!' He waved the piece of paper about like a white flag. 'Roger Jenkins! I found one. There are a ton online, but there was one sticking in my mind. It didn't jump out at first, because it says at the top "Mr R. Jenkins", but his name is at the bottom. Roger Jenkins.'

'Who is he? A member of the fight club you just joined?'

'No, he's my orthopaedic surgeon. I just saw him yesterday. Christ, why didn't I remember him?'

Lillian shot out of her chair so fast that Skellett genuinely thought she was going to run over and batter him. 'Get control or somebody way higher up to contact the NHS. We need to know where that bastard lives.'

'Why?'

'Don't you see, Charlie? Kenny Smith and Billy Ferguson were posed using metal plates and screws and all sorts of braces. The sort of thing an ortho surgeon might know about.'

'Jesus,' Skellett said, getting on the phone.

FORTY-TWO

The plane landed at Edinburgh Airport and the cars were waiting with motorcycle outriders, thanks to Davie Ross making a phone call from his bed, with the help of Joan Devine, who dialled the number for him.

'Orkney and back in a day,' Angie said from the back of the Volvo patrol car as it hammered along the Edinburgh Bypass with all its bells and whistles going. 'As sightseeing trips go, I've had worse.'

'Not something that's going to be happening again anytime soon,' Stewart said. 'Except maybe to Evans. Just before we left, he hinted that he wanted to be stationed up there permanently.'

'Did he?'

'In a roundabout sort of way. It's how I inter-preted his remark.'

The driver took the Calder Road exit and soon they were heading up towards Gillespie Crossroads.

'The road's been sealed off at either end,' Harry said. 'Silent approach,' he told the driver, who cut the siren when he was halfway through the lights.

There was tape across the road and a uniform lifted it for them to get through.

'Entry team are on standby, just waiting for the word to go,' Harry said, reading a text from Lillian O'Shea, who was on the scene with Charlie Skellett.

'See if that fucker's hurt Lynn...' Stewart said. The driver looked in the rearview mirror. 'He'll go to prison for a very long time.' *And he'll fucking die there.*

The car pulled into the side of the road. Uniforms were on either side, with Armed Response in front of them. Harry, Stewart and Angie jumped out of the car after it stopped.

Stewart wasted no time.

'Breach that fucking door!' he shouted.

The uniform with the red ram ran through the gate past the high hedge atop the wooden fence. Dr Roger Jenkins' house.

It didn't take much to breach the lock on the door

and then the armed officers were inside, shouting, threatening, telling anybody inside they were going to get their fucking bollocks blown off if they had a weapon.

Nobody did. The detectives waited outside until the house was swept.

'Nobody here, sir,' the armed team leader said. 'But you need to have a look down in his basement.'

They followed him down the stairs into a well-lit room that looked like an operating theatre.

'Some guys settle for a large-screen TV,' Angie said, 'but this bastard settles for an operating table.'

'This looks like where Kenny Smith was murdered,' Harry said.

'And Billy Ferguson,' Stewart added.

'No, Ferguson was murdered in Kenny Smith's house. There was a bedroom that looked something like this, with blood and bolts in it.'

There was blood on the floor and on towels that sat in a hamper.

'If he's hurt Lynn, I swear to God I'm going to fucking hurt him,' Stewart said.

'Get in line, Calvin,' Angie said.

'Right behind you, chief,' Harry said. This room was making him feel sick.

Lillian came down the stairs. 'Yes! We got a hit

from Works and Pensions. A friend of mine works in Customs, and he managed to do what he does best and...well, let's just say he got the info. Dan Jenkins has only been working with the estate agency for six months.'

'Good work, Lil,' Stewart said, 'but we could have asked that woman he works with for that information. What's her name again?'

'Catriona Taylor.'

'Aye.'

'She's out for the evening. Lives with her mother, doesn't have a boyfriend, is out on the lash in the centre of Edinburgh, so this was the next best thing.'

'Good job,' Stewart said, patting her on the arm. 'Now we know that the wee bastard's been floating about. But where is he now?'

Lillian was looking at her phone. 'I'm not finished, sir. Dan Jenkins also has a part-time job.'

'Christ. Do you know where?'

'You're not going to believe this.'

FORTY-THREE

Of course the place was shut, but that didn't mean they couldn't take the lock off the back door. They weren't going to fanny about waiting for somebody to come out and unlock it for them.

'I want to go in,' Stewart said.

'I know you do,' Angie said, 'but let me and Harry do this. Miller, Elvis and Skellett are all here. Lillian too. Plus all the uniforms. Let me and Harry deal with it, okay?'

'Just one little kick at the fucker.'

'You're not concentrating right now, Calvin. We need to focus, for Lynn and Julie's sake.'

'Okay, okay. Go get the bastards. But we'll be very close by.'

'Don't worry, pal, if Lynn and Julie are in there, we'll get them back.'

Angie led the way along the corridor, Harry close behind. The alarm system company had been working with them to shut down the system, and it had worked.

They moved silently along some corridors, past doors that led into rooms but were locked.

They'd had a quick look at the schematics for the building on a laptop, and Harry had never felt so focused in his life.

Then they were into one of the back galleries. It was open to the ceiling with landings running around the periphery on each floor.

'I've never been in this museum,' Angie said in a quiet voice.

'You should visit again when we're not so busy.'

They walked quietly into the corridor they wanted, Harry remembering that the workshop was just around the corner. They could hear noises coming from behind rubber doors: banging, hammering, drilling.

'Oh, Christ,' Harry said, and rushed at the rubber doors, flinging them wide open.

Julie Stott was unconscious on a hand truck, tied

to it with rope, her mouth gagged, and her head flopped forward.

Roger Jenkins looked up first and threw a heavy wrench at Harry, who ducked, but then Roger threw a bin at him.

'Danny!' Roger shouted as he ran for a door, slamming through it. Harry was after him.

Angie saw Dan, the younger one, the one she had been told about. He was at the far end of the room, near another door, and he opened it and ran through.

Angie saw a figure under a white sheet and she grabbed hold of it, yanking it off. Lynn McKenzie was underneath, gagged and tied to the table. Angie pulled the gag free.

'Go get them, Angie. Those bastards.'

Angie cut the ropes first and saw Lynn sit up as she ran after Dan Jenkins, aka Desperate.

Harry heard footsteps running up the stone steps ahead of him and chased up after them. Then the sound of a door being opened and then, nothing. He was breathing heavily as he caught the door as it was slowly closing on its automatic arm.

He stepped through into a corridor and then it was as if he was just a visitor. Muted light shone from an emergency exit sign and Harry looked over to where the *Dr Who* exhibition was. This Tardis had two doors and one of them was swinging slowly closed.

Of course he'd seen the films where the bad guy just pushed a door to make it look like he had gone through it, but the place was vast, and if Roger Jenkins had indeed done that, then God knows where he had gone.

He took his phone out and sent a text to Stewart. *Get in here! Dr Who.*

He gently pushed through the door and into the exhibition, putting on the torch on his phone, sweeping the light around. He saw what visitors saw when they came in: the robot dog, aliens, models, blown-up photos. He turned a corner and saw the story timeline going from the early sixties onwards. There were Daleks, and what looked like a statue from a cemetery. He wished he had watched more of the show.

He swept his light around some more and then stopped. There was a life-size model of Tom Baker, complete with hat and scarf. Roger Jenkins had modelled himself on this character, adding a beard and glasses so he could be Tom Powers, from an old James Cagney film. The name Eddie Bartlett, too. Another name from a Cagney film.

Harry walked towards the model and shone his light on the face. He took the light off and then felt arms go round his chest and he struggled as *Dr Who* stepped off the display and pointed a knife at his eyeball.

'Now then, who have we got here? McNeil, isn't it?' Roger Jenkins said. 'Charlie Skellett talks very highly of you.'

'They said Tom Powers was an old man,' Harry said.

'*Dressed* as an old man. Long coat, hat and scarf, fake beard and glasses. I'm an orthopaedic surgeon, I know how old men walk. I faked it, and rather well, even if I do say so myself.'

'You'll never get out of here,' Harry said as the arms released him. He turned to look at Dan Jenkins.

'That's a line from one of the Cagney movies,' Dan said, smiling. 'I can't remember which one now.'

'It doesn't matter, Dan. What matters is, we get away from here,' Roger said.

'I know that. Stop talking to me like you're my dad. You're a year older.'

'You told that copper bitch that I was your dad when I was in that wheelchair back at the house.'

'I had to tell her something, didn't I?'

'You could have said I was your brother, cheeky bastard.'

'We spoke to your mum and step-dad,' Harry said. 'Up in Orkney.'

'So?' Roger said.

Harry looked at him. 'So Morris told us he'd shot and killed Angus Smart. He showed us where he was buried. Beside the old man in the cemetery. In the old man's grave. The funeral you were at before they discovered Octavia.'

Dan came round to look at Harry and smiled. 'He did what?'

Harry nodded. 'He was coming to check on you all at your grandpa's house, just to make sure everything was okay, and he saw Angus coming out of your house. Then he took off after him in the car.'

'He thought Angus had killed Octavia?' Dan said.

'Shut up, Dan,' Roger said.

'No, he killed him because he was sleeping with his daughter,' Harry said.

'Wow. I didn't know the old fart had it in him,' Dan said.

Harry looked at Roger. 'Angus didn't kill your sister, did he?'

'No. That little tramp was having a good time with Kenny Smith and Billy Ferguson. Jelly Bean and Billy the Whizz, as we called them. We left our grandpa's house to go back and get some video games. We saw them leave, laughing and joking and saying what a slag she was. They wanted one last time with her before she left with the teacher. Then I heard Kenny say he had been sleeping with our mum.'

'Ruby hated Octavia, didn't she?' Harry said.

'Not hated her but was envious of her. She saw her youth slipping away so I think she jumped at the chance of sleeping with Jelly Bean. Kenny. But when we went in, Octavia was lying in her bed, barely dressed,' Roger said. 'I asked her what the hell she thought she was doing? She was supposed to be along at Grandpa's with us, but she said she was bored with the old films. She'd rather be in the house having fun, even though she wasn't meant to be there. She told us she hated us and was glad to be running away with the teacher,' Roger said.

'She taunted us,' Dan added. 'She said that Jelly Bean and Whizz were more men than we'd ever be.'

'Who killed her?' Harry asked. 'You or Dan here?'

Roger looked at Dan.

'It was me,' Dan said. 'Octavia had a knife on her bedside cabinet for opening her letters. I picked it up and stabbed her with it.'

'I tried to stop him but it was too late. He was frenzied. I wasn't going to let him go to prison for some girl who wasn't flesh and blood. We went back to Grandpa's house and the old boy was sleeping. We put in another Cagney film and woke him up, telling him he'd missed the end. He laughed and we got a beer and watched the next film. He never knew we'd been out. When the Glasgow detectives came, we said that Octavia must have slipped out as we were all watching the film. Grandpa was our alibi.'

'Very clever,' Harry said. 'But why kill Kenny Smith and Billy Ferguson?'

Roger gritted his teeth. 'Kenny came to see me as an outpatient. Some shoulder problem. I gave him an injection. He recognised me. We got talking and he told me that he was writing a memoir and Billy was helping. That the truth about what went on was going to come out.'

'And that angered you enough to kill them?'

'We didn't know if he actually knew about us

killing our stepsister or whether he was going to tell everybody he had slept with our mother. We didn't want to take a chance, but we just didn't want to throw him out a window or under a bus. It had to be exciting. So we recreated the crime scene.'

'And you thought you were just going to walk away?' Harry said.

'We did actually,' Roger said, then raised the knife. Harry caught it as it was brought down, then Roger let out a cry as the boot landed between his legs.

'I don't fucking think so,' Calvin Stewart said, stepping back as Roger went down to the floor, dropping the knife. 'That other wee bastard's running, Harry, but there are more of us in here now.' He smiled as he watched Harry roughly grab Roger's arm and turn the man over, slapping the cuffs on him.

'Sorry to rain on your parade, Harry, son, but I was getting impatient.'

'Means to an end, and all that,' Harry said.

FORTY-FOUR

Angie ran as fast as she could down a long corridor, Dan in her sights, but then he turned a corner. She was forced to slow down in case he was waiting to ambush her, but he wasn't there when she went round, preparing to fight.

She couldn't see him in this corridor, even though the lights were on. Two doors faced her as she raced up: stairs or staff only.

She pushed the stairs one, hoping to God he hadn't gone through here. She would rather fight than climb stairs. There was no option for going down, only up. She heard his shoes thumping on the stone steps leading up.

'Shite.' She went through the door and moved as fast as she could, getting up to the first level where the fire door was just about to close. She grabbed it and stormed through.

They were in a gallery with mannequins dressed up in clothes from different eras. She wandered round the glass cases, keeping her eyes open for Dan Jenkins, not seeing him, but expecting him to jump out at her. There was nobody there.

She stood and looked at one of the dummies. It looked like the same kind from the Edinburgh crime scene.

She took in a deep breath and moved around, her senses keen. She'd hated museums when she had been at school but going on a trip to one meant getting out of school for a half day. Otherwise, it had been years since she had stepped inside one, and she certainly hadn't been in this one.

She moved on, walking along the main level that overlooked the grand gallery below.

She moved in and out of a couple of smaller galleries but there was still no sign of Dan. Where the hell had he gone? If they couldn't find the brothers, they'd have to call in a swarm of Uniforms.

She found herself in the technology gallery, with old computers and electronics. She could make out a large model boat in a glass case, and an old telephone exchange.

Where the hell had he gone? She ducked down to try to see if he was hiding behind a display case but couldn't see him. She turned round. There were four planes hanging from the ceiling in an atrium, the very top one an old glider that looked like the wings were made of paper. She looked across to the other side of the gallery. He wasn't there.

Nobody was. Where the hell had Harry and that other mad twat gone? She saw Calvin Stewart reaching the top of the stairs and walking towards the *Dr Who* exhibition, then he disappeared out of sight.

She walked round the exhibitions, looking all around her. She walked back to the fire door she had come through. Maybe he had dodged her and had gone back downstairs? Surely she would have noticed him? Christ, this was frustrating.

She walked back the way she had come, looking round a large display case. Nobody there. He wouldn't have climbed the railings and dropped down to the level below, would he? No, surely it was too high.

She didn't see him silently running from the *Dr Who* exhibition into this gallery.

She looked round a display showing an old telephone exchange and another with some old computers.

Then she heard it, just the barest squeak, and it was this tiny noise that she would dream about afterwards. The squeak that saved her life.

She'd walked past the two phone boxes in her rush to see if Dan was hiding behind a case. He wasn't.

He was hiding in the red telephone box. The door squeaked when he opened it. She turned round to see him running at her, fully intending to push her over the edge of the balcony to the gallery floor below.

She sidestepped at the last second before he could push her, and too late he realised his mistake and hit the banister at full speed. Gravity took hold of him and threw him over the edge. He screamed for a second until he hit the glass case below, a piece of glass slicing into his neck.

It seemed that, unlike the planes hanging by wires, Dan couldn't stay in the air.

Figures rushed into the hall below.

Frank Miller looked up at Angie. She nodded to him just as Harry and Stewart dragged a moaning Roger Jenkins out of the exhibition.

FORTY-FIVE

Two days later, the team were in the Incident room drinking coffee, talking over the case, making sure everything was in order. Angie Fisher was with them; she was staying until everything was wrapped up. CCTV footage from the museum's security cameras showed that Angie hadn't laid a finger on Dan but had merely protected herself by stepping out of the way. Dan Jenkins was dead before the ambulance arrived, a piece of glass cutting his carotid artery.

Everyone stopped chatting when Lynn McKenzie walked into the Incident room. She smiled.

'Davie Ross is getting released today,' Stewart

said. 'I told him I'd be there for him and Joan to take him to...wherever he's going.'

'There will be an enquiry of course, but there's more than enough evidence for the Crown Office to throw the book at Roger Jenkins.'

'The house at Colinton, ma'am,' Lillian said. 'Who does it really belong to?'

'A businessman. The estate agent is also a Factor and they look after houses while people are away. The brothers decided to live in that one while the owner is away long term in Thailand. But Roger Jenkins took it one step further and created an operating room in the wine cellar. Jesus.'

'And to think he almost got his hands on me,' Skellett said. 'I mean when I was in his office.'

'I think you were quite safe,' Harry said. 'I mean, Julie was the one who got punched on the jaw.'

'How is she?' Skellett asked.

'Sore. Having a week off work to rest up. But she's fine.'

'All because Kenny Smith was writing his memoirs,' Stewart said. 'I never liked the man, politically.'

'I'm just glad you all got to me before I was stabbed, like Davie Ross was,' Lynn said. 'It was Dan who stabbed him. He blamed us for interfering back in Orkney all those years ago. The people on the island closed ranks and wanted to deal with the murder themselves. We investigated of course, but it went cold, then Davie Ross wanted it looked at again recently. That kicked things off, along with Smith's memoirs.' She smiled at Stewart. 'I'm going to the canteen for a cuppa if anybody wants to join me,' she said.

They all did.

'It was nice working with you, Angie,' Harry said.

'Likewise, Harry. I'm sure our paths will cross again.'

'I hope so.' He left the Incident room and the only two left there were Stewart and Angie.

'You did well there, Angie,' Stewart said.

'You too, old yin.'

'Shut up.' He smiled at her. 'If it doesn't work out in Fife, you could always go back to Helen Street. I'm sure Davie Ross would put in a good word for you.'

'He said the same thing when I called him this morning. Hey, you never know. Never say never.'

'Let me ask you one thing, though: did that wee trip to the museum turn you into a *Dr Who* fan?'

'I didn't get to see the exhibition, remember? Somebody was too busy making me try to catch a plane...'

AUTHOR'S NOTE

First of all, I'd like to give a huge shout out to a friend of mine for all his help, and for giving me technical advice. He doesn't want to be named, but you know who you are.

Thank you to my wife and family for their continued support. And to Charlie Wilson. I don't know how she does it, and comes out in one piece on the other side.

A huge thanks also to Jacqueline Beard, from a very grateful author.

Thanks also to Angie Fisher.

Finally, thank you to you, the reader. If I may ask, if you have a spare minute, could you please write a review on Amazon, or give this book a rating. I hope you enjoyed reading this one.

Harry will return in *Twist of Fate* which will be available to pre-order very soon.

Take care my friends.

John Carson
New York
April 2023

Made in the USA
Las Vegas, NV
17 April 2023

70744797R00203

They're rich. They're powerful. They're dead.

Settling into his new life, Detective Chie
Inspector Harry McNeil is being kept busy, bu
life is going to become a lot busier.

The body of an MSP has been found slaughtere
in an empty house in Edinburgh. But this is n
ordinary crime scene. It's one that Harry McNe
thinks he's seen before. Down to the last deta
including the position of the bodies.

As they start the hunt, they're looking for a kill
who seems to know far too much detail of wha
goes on behind the scenes at a kill sit
Somebody who doesn't want to stop.

Then Harry recollects where he saw this crim
scene before.

This killer is copying murder scenes from th
past. But the past is very much going to catch u
with the present...

ISBN 9798390750483

9798390750483